mustache may

JON MEYER

ISBN: 1452869774
ISBN-13: 9781452869773

To the places of this story

It starts now—a month and half of furry, socially obtuse hair on my upper lip. The lead up to Mustache May is upon me. Why do I do this? I didn't lose a bet. In fact, I helped come up with the idea. Maybe it's because we're attention whores? Maybe we just want to get noticed in the wash of what the world has become? No, that's too heavy and deep, at least this early in the morning. How does the mirror fog up so quickly?

I swipe at a steamy reflection until I can see myself. Friends say that my face has aged, but when I look at photos from college I don't see it. I always thought I looked twenty-four when I was eighteen, so what's that make me now—thirty?

Moopy stumbles to the toilet for his morning piss. We share a toilet and shower, but have our own sinks and mirrors. He's in his standard gym shorts that are sagging below his ass, and no shirt. Moop just got a new job as a forensics accountant, but according to him, he spends most of his day playing solitaire. I met Moopy my senior year at Gonzaga through my main group of friends. He went to high school with my other current roommate, Hern, and would come to party in

Spokane what seemed like at least once a month. Of the five or six guys that would consistently visit, Moopy was my favorite. He's a jolly type fellow. Round face, eyes that squint when he smiles, and a belly that originated the same time he started drinking heavily.

Hern and I had been living in the Watermarke for eight months before we moved into a three-bedroom and added Moop into the fray. I had been originally looking to move completely out after chasing a dream job that was going to take me traveling across the country, allowing Moop to move into my vacant space, but it fell through leaving Moop on the outside until Hern brought up the idea of just moving into a three-bedroom that was available in the building. That was a year ago.

"Morning, Moop."

"Morning."

I close the door to deafen the sound of his heavy flow. Sometimes it wakes me up at night even with two doors between my bed and the toilet. He's not the cleanest of roommates, but it could be worse.

I grab the shaving cream that I took from Moopy's side of the aisle. He uses an electric razor. I have never used foam before this stuff. Like the mirror, the foam instantly dissipates once I wipe it on, and I grow concerned for my skin because I don't feel confident in the frothy foam protecting my face. It's a good face I think; straight lines, solid chin, remnants of freckles. The excess in my hands gets reapplied to lighter-looking areas, especially on my neck. That's where I cut myself the most. I'm going to bleed. Two weeks until May first.

I grab the razor from its resting spot in the brown coffee mug to my right. God, I hate shaving. The first strokes. I start just above my Adam's apple and with some pressure slide the razor up until stopping under my chin. From there, I move to my left and do the same. This stretch is always the most tender and vulnerable to cutting for some reason. I've devised a new theory, or plan of attack regarding this section: less pressure while in turn possibly giving up the closest shave. Four strokes and I'm cleaning my right jaw and edging my side burns. No blood on my neck yet—time for the other side. I scrape up just off the center until my jaw bone, and now, the great crevasse that is the right side of my neck. Cutting is not the issue here—no, no—it's the four little hairs that are always left after my first attempt that take a precise, angled swath along my sternocleidomastoid muscle. It's such a bother I looked it up.

Moop flushes the toilet and coughs on his way out. He needs to stop smoking; should probably stop chewing as well.

The cheeks are easy. I wipe the mirror again. My left hand moves to my chin for extra pull. Little chunks at a time in no particular order under my bottom lip. One broad stroke under the butt of my chin, and I'm finished.

I grab my brown hand towel speckled with bleach spots that I really should wash more, and wipe the remnant shaving cream off from my neck and ears. Beginnings of a pubescent mustache prickle with excitement.

The apartment door shuts. Moop got out of here fast. He must be late for his bus downtown. Nothing like the helpless feeling of chasing after a bus while seeing the driver's eyes in his side view mirror. I've found the act of chasing a bus also leaves oneself sweaty and unappealing for the day to come. I can't believe I used to play basketball in my school clothes before first period in middle school, and spend the rest of the day with dried sweat all over me. Simpler times? Probably not.

I grab my lime green boxers with the fern print from the towel rack and put them on, right leg first. My legs look bigger. The random bike rides are paying off. Leg and pube hair that I trimmed a couple of weeks ago is starting to grow back. Won't be a problem for another month or so. I've got a mustache to worry about.

I apply deodorant, face moisturizer, walk through the cologne my mother bought me, and leave the bathroom. Looking through the apartment's huge bay window, another borderline day in Seattle—partly cloudy with no chance of being warm, awaits my next move.

The first documentation of a mustache comes from an ancient nomadic people, the Pazyryk, *who occupied the Altai Mountains in Southern Siberia. Although shaving with stones was technologically possible during Neolithic times, visual confirmation was not seen until this ancient tribe produced the* Scythian Horsemen, *a felt artifact highlighting a young man, his horse, and his mustache.*

As rare as the Horsemen, *evidence of alternative styles is just as hard to find, confirming the evolution of the mustache as one of history's great mysteries.*

My chest is hurting again. I shove the letter away so my tears don't drip onto the pages. I've already rewritten it three times. I don't want to have to rewrite it again after finally getting down what I think she needs to hear. Get your shit together. Make the call.

"Hey."

"Hey."

"So can I come up to your place?"

"Why would you do that? The Element's still in the shop, right?"

"Want to meet halfway, then?"

"Why don't I just come to your place?"

Because it's shitty to have you come over here for me to break up with you, and then have you drive home. I think it's rude.

"Um...OK. That's fine."

"See you in a few."

"OK."

Fuck.

I'm leaning against my bedroom door frame when J-Bird enters. I'm waiting for her the same I way I would when she'd come over after her shifts at the hospital. The letter is in my hand.

"It's easier for me to write, but you know that. I'll answer any question you want."

J-Bird takes the three pages out of my hand without taking her eyes off mine, and sits down at the computer desk. I move to the kitchen and lean on the counter, and wait for the inevitable eruption. Her eyes dart across the pages, but reveal nothing from within. Once finished, she throws the pages on the desk.

"You really want to break up? You have to be fucking kidding me! That's pretty rash, Jon."

Calm. Act calm. You've thought this out.

"I've been thinking about it for a while. It's not like this is a spur-of-the-moment type of thing."

"And once again you don't feel the need to tell me that, what, let's see here, you don't love me anymore? Never felt like something you might want to bring up?"

"It's the first time I've gone through anything like this, and I wanted to make sure I knew what I was feeling and that I made the right decision. That took time to figure out."

"So you were just waiting for it?"

"It's not like that. To me, we've hit a plateau the last four months. I can't help but think of you more like a friend at this point."

That sounds stupid.

"Well that's what good relationships are...friends who happen to be a little more."

"So friends with bennies?"

"Don't be stupid. Do you still love me?"

I cross my arms, preparing for the blow.

"Not anymore."

"Is this because I brought up Portland yesterday?"

"No...kind of...it made me think about things a little more seriously. I don't know if I'm moving to Portland yet, but I think it's a problem that not only did I not want to bring it up with you, I don't want you to come with me. Don't you think that's a problem?"

"I think you put too much weight in the effect your decisions have on me."

"Maybe I do, but nonetheless...what happens if I go to Portland and you come, and then we break up? I'm going to feel guilty as hell because I brought you down there, and then we're both stuck."

"I have a choice too, Jon. If I went it's because I wanted to go. Not just because you're down there. Who says I'd go to Portland anyways? I have things I want to do here."

"Personally, I'm not ready to be responsible for someone else's major life decisions. Maybe I overvalued your commitment?"

"Enough with the financial language!"

"I can't fucking help it, J-Bird. This is how my dad..."

"I know, I know. Your dad never had emotional conversations with you, and now you have a hard time with these things. I know, Jon."

"I'm sorry, but I saw serious flaws with the fact that I didn't want you in Portland if I was in Portland."

 And the fact I want to go on a date with a certain girl in Portland.

"You want some water?"

"No."

"You want to sit on the bed? It's more comfortable."

"No, Jon. I don't want to sit on your fucking bed. I want a straight answer."

J-Bird stands from the chair, snatches the letter, and heads for the exit. We meet at the door.

"Do you want to be single? Do you want out of this relationship?"

"If you read the letter..."

"Do you want to be single?"

Yes. I'm sorry. Be honest. For the first time be honest. You can't protect her. You can't lie to her. You have to be honest.

"Yes."

J-Bird opens and shuts the door, taking the stairs quickly. I open the slammed door and yell down the stairwell, "Please read the rest of it!"

"What's the fucking point? Leslie will be over in fifteen minutes with your shit!"

Leslie calls and I meet her outside. It's raining. Of course it's raining. She parks alongside the Watermarke's curb, pops her silver Civic's trunk, and gets out of the car.

"I'm sorry about having you in the middle of this, Leslie."

"When have I not been in the middle of it, Jon?"

"Good point. Thanks for doing this."

"Didn't go well, huh?"

"You're here, aren't you?"

"She's not happy."

"You know how she is. A couple of days and she'll be calm again. Quite rational when emotion fades."

"I hope so."

"Me too."

I manage to get the box into my arms, say goodbye, and re-enter the Watermarke. It's a box of memories. A couple of pictures, some socks, and...shit—the matching necklace and earrings I bought her for Christmas. No diamonds or anything. One small hoop inside of another. Simple. Like us. Until now. This was a gift. I don't want this. It was a gift for her.

Bruising pain is erupting in my chest again, just below the bottom tip of my rib cage, and I begin sobbing again. Harder than I cried for Danae. Harder than ever before. I push my computer aside for my elbows, and let it come.

Why did you have to hurt her?

Hurt now saves a bigger hurt later.

Keep telling yourself that.

Riley greets us at the door. His marble eyes have gotten cloudier since the last time I visited. Chocolate Labs always have issues.

I follow Bill and Rosemary into the kitchen where Karyn is soaking some pasta. Phil emerges from his office down the hall.

"Hello, Meyers! And, Jon, so glad to have you home. The great traveler. When do you head back to Seattle?"

"Tomorrow. You know I can't stay anywhere more than two days."

I give Karyn a firm hug. She's in forest green sweats and a multicolored striped sweater. Fantastic. Her cooking is being assisted by a glass of Pinot.

"Such a busy boy."

Phil and I shake hands. His hair is shorter than usual. New glasses too.

"Missed you on the ridge today, Phil."

"Ah, I had some papers to correct."

"The life of a Heritage College professor."

"And now the new dean of the Science Department."

"That's a proud wife you have."

"It's really just a title."

"Well congratulations, Dean."

Riley is feeling his way around the kitchen by grazing his head into cupboards.

"The pasta is almost ready to go. Why don't you guys head into the dining room and get set."

The group follows orders because that's what you do with Karyn, and filters into the dining room. Karyn, I'm assuming, has framed the photo I gave them of the lighthouse in Bandon. That's nice. With more chairs than people, we choose to occupy the south half of the table. Wine glasses are filled.

I'm working on my second piece of bread when there's a silence, and the inevitable question from Karyn is finally aired:

"So, Jon. How's J-Bird doing?"

And here comes the disappointment.

"Um...she's good. We broke up, but, well...we're still talking, which is good."

Pause.

"Oh, I'm sorry. What happened?"

Karyn's a psychiatrist so she'd know if I was dodging.. The truth is always better with her, and I usually get some pretty good advice in turn.

"I've been thinking about moving to Portland, just to make the job a little easier, and in that equation I never really considered J-Bird, or wanted to have her move with me. I saw that as a big issue. Being twenty-four I think I should only be with someone if I see marriage as a future, and since I didn't...don't want J-Bird to come to Portland I took that as a sign. We weren't really advancing as a couple, kind of at a standstill. Of course, I also want to date some other people before signing up for the big push."

Phil places his fork on the half empty plate in front of him, and places his elbows on the table, clasping his hands together.

"So Jon, did you ever talk to J-Bird about your intentions of moving to Portland, before the big talk?"

"No. Nothing was set in stone yet, so I didn't want to bring it up unless I knew I was for sure going to be moving."

Phil breaks his hands apart and raises them above his head in expected disbelief.

"Well there you have it. You're a young man acting with youthful cunning. Soon you will understand that women want to know everything you're doing, present and future. Good communication is the key to success in all walks of life."

"OK, I think I understand."

"It sounds like you've made a very mature decision, and put lots of thought into it. So how'd the breakup talk go? Was she receptive or emotional?"

Emotional is one way to put it. I'm not hungry anymore.

"Oh, very bad. I'm so awful at those sorts of things. I wrote her a letter explaining my position because that's what this damn book she gave on how to be a good boyfriend said to do if you're not a great emotional talker."

My father and Phil are looking down at their plates, nodding.

"After some back and forth, she stormed out and sent Leslie, you remember Leslie from last summer, ten minutes later to return everything I had in her house including the necklace and earrings I bought her for Christmas."

"Oh dear. Are you OK?"

Are you OK?

"Yeah, I think so. That hurt. They were gifts, it's not like I'm going to give them to someone else. They're just in a drawer now."

You're OK.

"I've already been on a couple of dates. It's nice not feeling guilty when talking to a random girl."

"You know me and your mother thought the world of her, but you're still our favorite."

I still think the world of her too. That's the problem.

"In your professional opinion, Karyn, am I going to be OK?"

She takes her time with an answer, enjoying a sip of wine first.

"The fun is in finding out."

Perfect.

"Hey, Holdz, Jesse at your place yet?"

"Yeah, all the way up from LA the bastard made it. You know how to get to my place?"

"Nope, just give me the address. I'll get directions on the Internet."

I scribble quickly as Holdzworth offers directions.

"Cool, got it. See you in a couple of hours."

"Bring your drinking pants."

"Will do. Late."

I get out of my car, cross the sidewalk, and take in Lake Union and the skyscrapers behind it in all their glory. This Wallingford has something going for it. Time for meet and greets. Something along the lines of, "What have you been up to?" or "How's the job?" All the standard shit. Don't be so negative. Tonight will be fun. Before I can knock, Justin opens the door. He hasn't changed since school ended. It has only been two months. What did you expect? His thin hair is neatly arranged to look messy. He's wearing a fairly stylish button-up shirt with thin jeans, and Diesel-type-looking shoes—Justin's standard away-from-work wardrobe. Although he's a stair up on me we're almost eye to eye. Hands are shaken.

"So, you found it all right?"

"Yeah, no problem, getting the hang of Seattle. Too bad I have to go back to Spokane soon and forget all of it." He turns back into the entrance and I follow.

"Those turnabouts are fucking annoying."

"I know, but like the traffic, you get used to them."

"Sure," I say, not really concentrating on the conversation, making sure I don't trip on the steep, ill-lit stairs. We get to the top of the stairwell and Justin opens the door letting light into the hallway. I can see some of his apartment, and I catch a glimpse of Jesse's oversize, white shoes. The door swings fully open and I walk into what looks to be a living room where Jesse is laying on couch, watching TV with his luggage bags below him. Jesse rises and smiles.

"Heeeeeyyyy, Meyer!"

"Golds, good to see ya, man."

"Well you know, I couldn't let you kids have all the fun in Seattle without a visit from Uncle Jesse."

"Right, right." We awkwardly lock hands and half hug.

"Well I couldn't let a night where I have two old roommates getting together pass me by."

Nothing has really changed with Jesse either. He's sporting baggy jeans, a horizontal, thick-striped pink and blue Polo brand shirt with a gold chain, and those fucking white shoes that I can see are Air-Force Ones. The earring in his left ear lobe still looks like someone shot him with a BB. In the three and a half years that I've known him, Jesse has always had the same short, classic Greek haircut.

"I'm glad you came up. Justin and I actually haven't seen each other yet this summer. We're both too busy sitting in cubicles on opposite sides of the city."

"That can happen, that can happen. Let's not ruin all the conversation right now. Uncle Jesse brought some top-shelf shit to enjoy on the roof."

I look to Justin.

"On the roof?"

"Yeah, on the roof."

I get distracted by a door creaking and catch a glimpse of a girl putting her chestnut hair into a pony-tail. The door shuts. The sun is almost set.

"We're not supposed to go up there, but tonight's a special night."

"So what do we have for booze? I just brought some beers."

"Follow me, Meyer, this is gonna be better than Chua's graduation party."

"I don't know, Jess." I take my eyes off the door and look back at Jesse. "A thousand dollar tab is pretty hard to beat."

The three of us move into the kitchen. Out the bay window, Lake Union rests peacefully under the I-5 bridge. The setting sun is lighting downtown on fire. Jesse reaches above white cabinets with circular blue knobs and grabs two large, oddly shaped bottles.

"Let me introduce you to my friends Hennessy and Hypnotic."

"Jesus, Jesse, you're some kind of gangster," Justin says and I think. I'm a beer guy. I have no idea what either of these things are, so I ask Jesse and he gives me a response that I still don't register because I can't take my eyes off the bottle that looks like it's glowing with radioactivity. I think it's the Hypnotic.

"You boys just set up the roof, and I'll take care of the drinks," Jesse assures us.

Justin and I move past him and into the back hallway. There's a set of stairs that lead to a back door, but Justin moves across the walkway, reaches up, and unhooks what looks to be an attic door. On his tiptoes, he pushes and the door rises into darkness. Justin then grabs the folding chair to my left and uses it to stand on so he can lift himself through the hole. Looks like he's done this before.

"Hand me up the rest of the chairs."

I look left and three more aluminum folding chairs are resting against the wall. One at a time we get them through the attic door, and onto what I'm guessing has to be the roof. I can hear Jesse singing to himself back in the kitchen.

"Come on up," says Justin's voice from the dark hole.

"All right, any tricks I should know about?"

"Naw, you just have to use your upper body strength."

"Yeah, sure."

I do as I'm told and throw my arms through the hole, locking my elbows on the roof, and push myself through. I brush off whatever might have accumulated on my clothes from the ascent before looking up, and take in the Seattle skyline. It seems so much closer than when I parked. Reflections of skyscrapers' lights reach all the way across Lake Union, ending only because the street begins. The three chairs I passed Justin through the hold are lined up beside each other facing the city. Justin is standing with his hands in his pockets taking in the young night.

"Wow."

"I know. I try to get up here as much as possible."

"Not much time left, you gotta do this every day, man."

"It does beat the cubicle."

"Yes, yes, it does."

We both chuckle to ourselves out of mutual empathy. Something is rustling near the hold.

"Hey! Somebody come grab these drinks!"

I wander back to the door in the roof and grab the three glasses Jesse is holding up to me. Once I've set them down, I grab just above his elbow and pull him through the hold. Jesse straightens, brushes off, and joins us in the scene.

"Holy shit."

Justin and I say in sync, "Yeah."

I hand out the drinks and the three of us plop down into the creaky folding chairs. I take a sip from my glass. This fucking tastes awful.

"Golds, what's in this… thing? It tastes like shit."

"No, my friend, it tastes like Hennessey and Hypnotic. The drink of choice for every rapper on the West Coast."

"Well, I'm not a rapper and I stand by my opinion that this tastes like shit." I look deeply into my glass and mumble, "but I'm still going to drink it."

Justin is sitting quietly sipping on his *Hennessey and Hyp*, apparently not seconding my opinion.

"So what are you up to, Meyer?"

"Well, Jess, I'm interning for Helly Hansen North America. It is what it sounds like. Shit. I'm the guy who fixes the copier, breaks the computer, and ships whatever you need shipped. I can't complain too much though. I get to wear what I want to work. I don't have to shave. I've got a pretty decent-looking lady boss that likes to hug. The CEO and I are golf buddies. I guess it's as good as corporate life could be. You?"

"Working for my dad again. LA is all right. Great clubs. Just expensive. He's putting me in contact with some people in Phoenix. I think I'm going to go into real estate."

"I could see you doing that," Holdzworth throws out.

"How 'bout you, Justin—what's Seattle offering you?"

Holdzworth leans forward and rests his chin into his hands.

"I work for the IRS. I can't believe it. I have to show a badge while walking through a metal detector to get into work. Governmental bureaucracy is brutal."

Even in the fading light, I can see the disinterest in his eyes.

"Sounds like you've had a longer summer than I."

"The difference is you two get to go back to school. I'm officially in the real world," he sits back up, "signed up and committed. Life's not over, but a lot of the fun walked out the door when I accepted that diploma."

I was hoping we wouldn't get too speculative tonight. It might lead to Jesse talking about his recently made ex-girlfriend.

"Well, you can live vicariously through Jesse and me for the next eight months. I think we're going to have a good run as seniors," I offer, not even really believing it myself. I quickly go to my drink, and wince again. Each of us gets through three cocktails before finally leaving the roof and skyline. We've decided on a bar on South Lake Union. We mosey back into the living room after barely surviving the descent from the roof, laughing and smiling about when Jesse got into a fight on Halloween dressed as a female tennis player, and there's the most adorable thing sitting on the couch. After the laughter drowns, Justin speaks up.

"Jesse, Jon, this is A-bomb. She's one of my room-mates. Still coming out with us?"

A-bomb nods and smiles.

"Hi, A-bomb, I'm Jon."

I grab my samples and leave Corporate for Evo before I can be pulled into an office and questioned about why I'm not calling on my accounts. I have to get rid of these samples. I'm going to owe Debi a ton of money if I don't sell more. The kids at Evo should come through.

Traffic isn't bad on 90. The Dodge Caravan rental is maneuvering well today. The End is playing another fucking Nirvana song. Is it blasphemous to say I dislike Nirvana? What about, "I can't stand Nirvana and I feel the city of Seattle feels somehow indebted to them, so they must play at least fifty of their songs a day"?

These words can never be said aloud. I change the radio to the pop station. That's sad.

I pull up in front of Evo and fit the van into a compact spot near the entrance. I'm not hauling these samples farther than they need to go. I pop the trunk and get out of the vehicle. The four blue garment bags are strewn about the back. I grab the rolling racks first and put them together before wheeling them up to the door. I place one of the racks against the door to keep it open, and slide the other into the store. Tom's at the cash wrap. The store lights are unusually low.

"Jonny, what up? Oh, you brought us the goods to look at."

"That's right, Thomas, get out the wallet. Helly Hansen's winter '08 line is here."

Moreno's wearing jeans and a T-shirt that are a full size too big as usual. Looks like Leslie bought him a new Mariner's hat. For being a slight fellow, he sure wears baggy clothes.

"Hey, give me a hand. Can you grab a couple of the garment bags from the van?"

"The van? Where's the Element?"

"Uh, I decided to wreck it. It's still in the shop. Don'l ask."

"All right, all right."

I'm so tired of answering questions about the fucking Element. This job has cost me so much money. Tom comes back into the store with a couple of garment bags.

"Just throw them on the rack. Thanks, man."

"No worries, I'm just pumped to see some new HH, you know, considering I don't work for them anymore."

"I know, I know. Still pissed after a year?"

"You know who can kiss my ass."

"Might be time to move on Tommy? C'mon, unzip those bags while I grab the others."

By the time I've brought the other bags in, Tom's set the rolling rack in the gallery. Some of my old Evogear co-workers bounce down the stairs from the corporate loft above the store. In the three months I worked here, I never really felt like one of them. They have this aura about them that comes off as too cool for school. Still, they're all very nice and mean well. Ah, there's Molly. She's a short little Asian chick who is really into photography and film too, but who isn't these days.

"Hey, Molly. Thanks for setting this up."

"No worries. After hearing you talk about the gear I had to get a look at for myself. The jacket and pants you hooked Tre' up with are sick."

Tre' and I were colleagues in the Merch Department together, and have kept a weird pseudo friendship since I've stopped working here. Evo people are now circling the clothes, randomly trying on garments. Molly and I had e-mailed back and forth the previous day to lock down a time so that everyone knew I was coming. I'm two hours late.

"Well, thanks again. Let me grab that jacket that I was telling you about."

I move between some former co-workers and smile politely because I can't remember names. Of course I remember most, but some are slipping my mind. There are also some new people grazing. I can't believe they're still hiring more people. I grab the plaid print component jacket for Molly. Just enough edge and style for her without going over the top.

"All right, throw this on."

I hand the jacket to Molly. Her face smudges.

"Uh, I don't know, Jon."

"Just try it on."

Molly accepts the jacket and heads to the bathroom for a mirror. Ben the Computer Guy has found some base-layer he likes. A bearded dude is fondling some fleece.

For clarification I shout," Just so you guys know, all the women's stuff is size medium and the men's is size large!"

Nods.

Molly comes back around the corner from the bathroom holding the jacket in her hands. Following behind her is a petit blonde—well, highlighted blonde—that takes me by surprise. She's cute. Has to be around twenty-three or twenty-four. Molly hands me the jacket.

"Sorry, Jon, just didn't fit right."

"Um, yeah. Well...take a look through the rest of the stuff."

I'm distracted and it's obvious. Molly clues in.

"Oh, you probably haven't met our new intern." The blonde perks up. "She's actually doing the same job you used to." The subject of Molly's and my discourse makes her way over.

"Hey, Meyer, how much for this jacket?" Tom yells from the other side of the room.

"Hundred. You're not going to buy it anyways, so why you even asking?"

"You're right," Tom mumbles to himself. I quickly refocus because the blonde and her fantastic athletic body are standing next to me. She's got crisp blue eyes.

"I'm Breezy. You used to be an intern here?" Molly peels off and starts looking at the other jackets.

"Yeah, I was in the merchandising department. Wrote descriptions for a lot of the Web product. Is that what they have you doing?"

"Uh huh, just started. This is my first week. I'm already feeling sapped on ideas."

"Oh, it doesn't get any easier. In the beginning you think you're so clever with all these funny anecdotes that you come up with, but soon enough the well runs dry and you stare at the screen searching for something creative to pop into your head, and then you just stand up and walk around the office to look like you're doing something. Can't say I miss it."

"Wow, you have it down."

"I don't think so. They didn't hire me so maybe they were looking for someone with an endless, creative well. Filling the gap?"

"I hope so, it sounds tough," Breezy offers with a cute smirk. That's her name right? Breezy? Shit, I forgot. Focus.

"In the meantime you should try on this jacket. Only a hundred bucks." I hand her the plaid jacket Molly just tried on.

"For sure, I'll be back in a second." Let's stick with Breezy, turns the corner for the bathroom. How does this happen? Two weeks out of a relationship and all I want to do is chill. I don't want to see hot girls right now. Well that's not true, but you do need to get J-Bird, and the fact that you still really want to have sex with J-Bird, out of your head. This is what you wanted. You wanted to be single. You wanted to be able to talk to girls without guilt. Deal with it. There's no going back. I hope she doesn't notice my stache stubble. Fucking Mustache May.

My eyes move back to the room and catch Tom watching her from around the corner. He realizes that he's staring and glances back at me, and I mouth, "Wow."

He mouths back, "I know," and starts to have imaginary sex with the air in front of him. I make some quick sales, maybe $80 worth of base-layer, and Blondie comes back around the corner wearing the jacket.

"I'll take it. It fits perfectly."

"Oh, really? It's a medium...I would have put you at a small. Whatever, well that'll be a hundred bucks."

Play it cool.

"Here's the thing, I don't have my checkbook on me. Can I pay you on my next shift?"

Of course you can, you beautiful thing.

"Of course you can. Let's see, I can pop in on Monday. Do you work then?"

"Yeah, Monday, Wednesdays, and Fridays. I start at twelve."

"Huh, that was my old schedule. OK, Monday, then."

You beautiful thing.

For January, the store is slow. We should at least be absorbing more returns. Leslie is finishing up her Nordstrom chicken sandwich behind the sunglass cabinet while I've been tasked as the greeter. I'm hungry. Tom is helping a customer over in the corner. She's looking to replace base-layer with what looks to be a rain jacket. He's really selling it. When she turns her back he winks at me. Up-sell, Tommy, up-sell.

"Happy to be finished up at Evo?" Leslie asks from behind me.

I turn to her and walk between a couple of fourways before leaning against the cash wrap. She could care less about my leaning. She goes for the "friend" managerial style, and it works for us.

"Yeah, I was getting really bored. Once I cashed in my intern credit it was hard to keep working, ya know?"

Leslie's a history major at the U. We've hung out a couple of times, gone to some movies. She's quite the fashionista for having to obey a dress code at The HH. She's pushing the new trend of tights under a jean skirt along with a Helly Hansen sweater. She's single as well. Most of our time is spent exchanging college stories or sex theories. It's a fine line we've been walking to not give up anything too personal.

Lyndsay comes out from the back. She fixes sleeves on a couple of jackets while making her way to the cash wrap.

"Jon! Stop leaning on the counter. Why aren't you up front?"

"C'mon, Lyndz—nobody is coming in."

Her face relaxes upon acceptance of my statement. Lyndsay concedes.

"Fuck. I hate days like this. I can't believe we have to stay till nine o'clock. Hey, I've already talked to Tom about this, but my friend Alexis is having an '80s party tonight. You guys want to come?"

Leslie and I look at each other and nod.

"I'll bring a couple of my roommates," Leslie offers.

"Think Hern will want to come, Jon?"

"Naw, he and Jacki are having a date night. Alexis is your friend from Boise, right?"

"Yeah, she just got a PR job here. I haven't been to her house yet, but I think she's pretty close to you."

"Near Wallingford? Nice."

Leslie's roommates, Alexis, I'm finally starting to meet some new girls. Things with Angie are going nowhere and shouldn't be after New Year's.

Tom's ushering his customer over to the cash wrap for a completed sale. The three of us move into women's section and lock down the plans for the evening. Leslie and roommates will pick up Lyndsay, and head to my place where we'll pre-funk before heading to the party. I'm looking forward to this.

I buzz the girls into the Watermarke. My checkered pants were just where I left them in the back of closet. I'm also sporting an old gym T-shirt with my best impression of Ducky's hair from *Pretty in Pink*. When the girls walk through the door, I stand from the couch. Leslie's dark brown hair is pulled into a side pony, and she has what looks like ten wristbands located about her body. Lyndsay looks like she's already been drinking. Maybe the bladder of boxed wine in her hand has something to do with it? Leggings not much different from what Leslie was wearing at work, accentuate Lyndsay's long legs before they go out of view under a pleather miniskirt. A stone-washed jean jacket is wrapped around her KISS tee. Lyndsay's shoulder-length, light brown hair has been burned and crimped. Following behind Lyndsay are Leslie's roommates, and a dude. I sip the Henry's Private Reserve in my hand waiting for introductions. I already enjoyed one beer in the shower. No sense in being bashful tonight.

"Girls, good to see you."

"Hey, Jon," Leslie replies, "this is my roommate J-Bird, Erin, and her boyfriend, Chris."

Hands are shaken with varying pressures.

"Nice to meet you guys, welcome to the Watermarke, although I don't think we'll be staying long. I have some cards if you want to play kings or asshole?"

J-Bird and Erin have moved to the kitchen and are preparing some cocktails for themselves. They look at each other and Erin replies, "I think we're just looking to get some drinks in us."

"No worries. The kitchen and its lack of amenities are at your disposal," I try at a joke. J-Bird, the brunette, offers a sympathetic smile. Good sign.

"Can we make you anything?" she asks.

"Nope, I'm good with my Weinhard's. Actually, could you grab me another one from the fridge, please?"

"Sure."

Leslie and Lyndsay flow to the living room, and join me on the couch. Out of courtesy to the girls, I punch off Sportscenter. In return, I receive approving looks. J-Bird and Erin finish making what looks like a couple of screwdrivers. Erin, wearing an array of pastel-colored tights, burrows her white, blonde hair into Chris' shoulder. He smiles and whispers in her ear. J-Bird approaches with my fresh Henry's. She's even taken the cap off. What a sweetheart. While she sips her screwdriver I take her in. Athletic body, larger than normal ass, but that's fine. She didn't go too crazy tonight with the outfit: Tight jeans, graphic tee, and a side pony keep the hoop earrings visible. A light raspberry lipstick brings out her lips, especially when she sips from her drink.

"I'm Jon."

"I know. Leslie's told me about you."

 Shit.

"Yikes, what about?"

"Just that you and Lyndsay went to school together. You like to have fun. You're fairly sporty."

I like the way she talks.

"Good enough start, I guess. Are you sporty?"

"I play soccer for the UW club team. Run a little. Just enough to not feel gross."

You don't look gross. Lyndsay yells that we should we leave, and everyone agrees. I turn back to J-Bird.

"Well, cheers to trying to stay in shape, or at least being conscientious about it."

"And to a good night."

"And to a great night."

We both drink and exchange smiles before exiting.

J-Bird and I stumble through the apartment door after a few drunken moments fidgeting with the key. Since the door was locked, Jeff and Jacki aren't home yet. Nice. We sloppily kiss on our way through the dark apartment to the bedroom, tripping on furniture, meandering our way around the corner into my room. Tongues, hands, ambitions are everywhere. We fall together onto the garbage mattress I got from Rusty for free. I love Rusty. I love J-Bird.

Twisting on my bed, I shove my hands under her T-shirt and lift, exposing a flat stomach and firm breasts. J-Bird lifts my shirt and throws it on my computer desk a good distance from the bed. Cars drive by on Stone Way outside the window. Her enthusiasm makes me smile. I take my checkered pants off and throw them into the back corner of my closet. I move to her jeans that look tighter in the dark. Kissing her stomach, I take them off along with her underwear in one motion. My mouth takes her for a couple of minutes before she touches the top of my head, and brings me back to her lips. J-Bird grabs me and I harden. Her body is incredible. My boxers slide off and I'm instantly inside her. It takes us both by surprise but she doesn't say anything. She's wet so it's easy. Going slowly, our rhythms match. My whole body is sensationalized, but I stop. She says it's OK, but I bashfully decline and roll over, smiling.

"Too soon."

Breathing heavily, "I know."

I say, "I know," and kiss her firmly so she knows I mean it.

APRIL 23ᴿᴰ / 2007 / SEATTLE

I can't believe I'm actually diagramming an outfit just to go to Evo. Well, Hot Blonde is also at Evo and you want to look good, don't you? How attractive can you look with a developing rat above your lip? Whatever, just go with the seersuckers and a pocket tee. I put on an outfit consisting of one of my many pocket tees and blue and white seersucker slacks. I bought these pants with J-Bird. She talked me into them. Was that the Crabfest trip? Maybe. Stop thinking about J-Bird.

I have no other business at Evo, so I leave my pack and laptop at home. I walk the ten or twelve blocks to Fremont because it's an unusually nice day. After eighteen years of walking with either a backpack or golf bag strapped to me, my back feels naked without something bouncing up and down.

Tom's not there when I show up at twelve, so I ask a couple of other shop guys if the intern has come in yet. I refrain from using the term, "Hot Blonde." Aware of whom I'm referencing, they shake their heads no. I climb the stairs to the mezzanine to look at what's on sale. Up here, I'll also be able to see when she gets in. Such a stalker. The white Reef sandals I bought last month have already gotten so dirty I could probably use another pair. They aren't matching up well with the white of my pants. My previous pair of Reefs lasted five years, and these will do the same.

I look up from my feet when I hear the door open across the store, and she walks in accentuated by the outside light. There might have been a fan blowing on her. She's wearing tight jeans and a pale yellow graphic tee, and sexy as hell heels. How does she... any girl wear those things? Amazing. I consciously take my time back down the mezzanine stairs to not look too excited. She sees me and smiles. That's good. I make my way between racks of clothes without tripping, and meet her at the bottom of the stairs leading to the corporate work space.

"Hey."

"Hey, you're a little late."

"I walked from SPU across the canal. Bridge was up, ya know?"

"Right, right. Shall we TCB?"

"Huh?"

"Sorry, take care of business."

Fuck.

"Yeah, sure, let's go upstairs."

"K."

Fuck.

She takes the lead up the stairs, which puts me right behind her beautifully shaped ass. Great calves too. Calm down. Play it cool. I say hi and hello, to Shilo and Sunny. They compliment me on Mustache May. Apparently, Tom spread the word through Evo and the

Men of Evogear are going to join in the fight. Finally, an inside joke that I started in this office.

Before I enter into the merchandising part of the office, I stop by Ben the Computer Guy's station and collect a check from him for the base-layer pieces he wanted. He's excitable as ever. Thanks, Ben.

OK, here we go. I walk through the French doors and she's already sat at her computer and busted out the checkbook.

"So one hundred, right?"

"Uh-uh, that will work." Small fingers frame a pen that fills in the blank lines. I glance at the upper right corner of the check she's now writing on. "Breezy Stills" it proclaims. Breezy. Shit, I was right. Well, if you were right you would have remembered. While she's writing, Tre' looks up from his computer. He's cut his hair but his beard has grown out. As usual, his camera is sitting next to his keyboard.

"Hey, Jon, what are you doing here?"

"Just collecting some fundage from when I brought the samples around last week."

"Oh, nice. Hey, check out these pictures I took from this weekend. I just met this chick and we spent all of Sunday running around."

I step around the desk to Tre's side, and lean down for a better view. Tre' maneuvers us through an album filled with random pictures of him and this girl. There are some pretty cool shots of the EMP mixed in. I look back to Breezy and my check is resting on the edge of her desk. She's opened up Photoshop. Looks like Sunny has her cleaning up images to be put on the Web site. Tre' finally gets to the end of the album. Where does he meet these girls?

"Nice pics, Tre'. I'll catch ya next time. Gonna work the stache', yeah?"

"You know this!"

"Sounds good, baby, late."

I take the five steps back to Breezy's desk and grab the check from the edge of the desk, say thanks, and anxiously head toward the French doors. That was too quick. Don't puss out. God, there are so many people around. Just fucking turn around. This is why you broke up with J-Bird. You wanted to be single so you could ask girls out. You wanted this.

I act like I forgot something and head back to Breezy's work station and squat with my hands placed on the edge of her desk. She averts her attention from the computer, and I lean in.

"Do you play tennis?" I whisper as to not bring too much attention, although everyone in the office knows exactly what I'm doing. Breezy doesn't match my hushed tone, and announces her answer.

"Funny that you ask. I actually played the other day, so yes is my answer."

"Would you like to play with me sometime?"

"Yeah," her eyes now moving about, "do you want my number?"

Jeez. This is too easy.

"Sure, sure."

I punch her number into my BlackBerry and stand up. That went fairly well.

"OK, well I'll talk to you later."

Breezy smiles, genuinely I think.

"OK."

"OK."

"What can I do for ya, Angie?"

"Shawnee, Matt, and I are going to get some dinner. You want to come?"

"Sure, where we meeting?"

"Matt's."

"Be there in five."

"OK. See you soon."

Good thing I just showered. I jump up from my mattress on the floor, but not so high that I hit my head on the ceiling. Just a couple of more months in this room. Only in the direct center can I stand completely erect without banging my head on a sloping ceiling. My computer desk to my left, I turn right and duck so I can get to my dresser. Thank God for Mom and Dad letting me use my old dresser this year, considering the rest of my clothes are in plastic containers in the hallway.

Is it shorts weather? I look out the two-by-two-foot window that is my only source of light in "The Cell," as I like to call it, and the late afternoon sun is still shining. I throw on my favorite white Nike gym shorts (because they have pockets) and my freshman year Kennel Club tee. I duck out of the room, scoop on my sandals, and head toward the staircase.

"Hey, Lark, you want to go to dinner?" I yell back down the hall before descending.

"I'm good," replies a muffled voice from behind his bedroom door.

"All right, catch ya later!"

He's probably rubbing. I duck my head and clear the last three steps. Devo and Woody's doors are closed meaning they aren't home. Who am I kidding? Even when they are home their doors are closed. I lock the house door behind me. Our yard looks like shit. I walk past Tesoro and cross Hamilton. A couple of blocks later I'm at Matt's place, which is right next to Shawnee and Angie's duplex on Mission. The screen door is still amazingly hanging on. The construction next to the house hasn't been kind to the current foundation. As usual, Matt's door is unlocked so I give a couple of quick raps and walk in. The kitchen is empty and dirty. Dishes sky out of the sink. Matt and Shawnee are laying on the couch in the living room watching TV.

"Where's Angie?" I inquire to the room.

"In the bathroom. Ready to go?"

"Yes, ma'am."

Shawnee peeks over the couch. "Yes, you are."

The TV restricts any answer longer than six words. Shawnee is obviously annoyed about something. Looks like she couldn't control the frizz today. Also, I'm sure she's not happy to be sharing dinner company with me and my anti-girlfriend propaganda that I continually feed Matt. Not in front of her of course. Angie has told me lay off, and I am. No sense going into graduation with any drama that isn't necessary. I just don't see the point of seriously dating someone. It's college. Especially for Matt and all the sophomores he's got hanging around this place because of Miller and Jimmy. I know that really pisses Shawnee off, but what can she do? Well, she can bitch. And she does.

Angie pops down the stairs from the bathroom. Looks like she's having a lazy day as well, wearing blue sweats and a red Gonzaga hoodie. She still looks skinny in baggy sweats. Her blonde hair is pulled back into a ponytail. She's been wearing her glasses a lot lately.

"Hey, what up?"

"Nothing, Angie, just hungry. Think we can get these lazy potatoes on the road?"

"Well, where we going, Jon Jon?"

"I was thinking South Hill. We haven't been up there in a while."

The three of them look at each other and nod.

"Then it's settled."

Shawnee and Angie leave the table after eating half of their burritos.

Matt observes, "I thought chicks could only go to the bathroom together in nice restaurants?"

"I don't know, man. When they want to talk they want to talk."

"They must be game planning for tonight. You know, how you and Angie and AREN'T going to hook up."

"Shut the fuck up. That's rude, uncalled for, and not even on the radar."

"What are you talking about, Meyer? You've wanted to grab Angie's little buns since sophomore year."

"Well so have you, and as we both know she's had a boyfriend or been still hung up on one ever since. Things have changed. We're doing the *friends* program now, dude. Hooking up in any form is off limits."

"So you're telling me that those nights you crash on their couch, right below her room, you've never thought about sneaking up into her bed and giving it a go?"

"She gives me the boot."

"What?"

"Yeah, man, well you know the only reason I crash there is 'cause I'm wasted, but I've never been so far gone to not know what I was doing. Every once in a while, I go up to Angie's room, I get in her bed, she mumbles, I don't make a move, and ten minutes later she kicks me out claiming that I'm snoring, which is most likely true."

"Wow."

"I know. I'm done trying. It's not worth wasting time on with only a month of school left. More juniors are starting to turn twenty-one and hitting the bars, and as you know, living close to the Triangle has its advantages."

"I haven't known those advantages in a while."

"Of course you haven't," I hesitate. "Nope, I'm not going to do this. I promised Angie I'd lay off."

"Why don't you promise Angie that you'll stop snoring?"

"Some things I can control—like my dick. My snoring is another subject."

"I wish I could control my dick."

"Well, Matt…when's it's as big as yours it can create problems. By the way, is the penis pump still in your golf bag?"

"Yeah, it's only a matter of time before I get busted by airport security."

"You know what's also a matter of time?"

"What?"

"When I bust in your face."

"Oh you'd like that, wouldn't you, you sick fuck? At least that would mean you were getting some."

I see the girls exiting the bathroom over Matt's shoulder. They're still laughing from their convo.

"And what were you ladies talking about?"

"Just how we're going to get you and Angie to hook up tonight."

Matt and I look at each other.

"Funny, same thing here."

Leading up to and through the medieval times facial hair was generally accepted in any form, partly because it was understood that the excess growth assisted with warmth during long winters. Experimentation in styling formats was encouraged even under the many monarchal societies throughout Europe.

One can assume, that the greater the beard, mustache, or growth in general, the greater the man.

MAY 1ST / 2007 / SEATTLE

It's a nice day. I'm on the roof of the Watermarke reading the latest *Esquire* with my shirt off to absorb any sun that will have me. I never read a full magazine, usually just Klosterman and the *Ten Things You Don't Know about Women* plug-in that ironically holds true to its title. There are a lot of things I don't know about women, at least ones that have a movie coming out. It can't be more than seventy degrees, but it feels like ninety. The deck of the Watermarke looks over the Seattle skyline from some distance, a nice highlight to a boring, cookie-cutter apartment complex. Someone has broken a tabletop on one of the patio tables, and the apartment manager hasn't gotten around to cleaning it up yet. I can't believe more people don't come up here. The traffic below provides a steady white noise ideal for reading.

It is also the first official day of Mustache May. Earlier this morning, I removed whatever growth was on my face and neck, leaving only a band of hairs above my upper lip. It's disgusting. It's perverted. It's Mustache May 2007.

It's also a Tuesday, meaning basketball after work for the Gonzaga contingent. Well, other people's work.

I'm of course enjoying the slow season for the outdoor industry, and have no significant time commitments related to work other than a few trips coming up. Debi took my samples back, at least the ones I haven't sold. She said I owe her only around twelve hundred, which is much less than I was anticipating. I need to double-check the order confirmation.

I pull the Element into St. Anne's Elementary at five past six o'clock. Scott, Gee, Jack, and Rado are already warming up. They live in the same complex on Queen Anne, so they move in units all while driving separately. A mini-armada of sorts. Scott looks like he's still losing some weight. Must not be eating out as much. I park alongside Rado's aging Lexus. I grab my pack from the passenger seat before getting out. The Mariners' game radio feed is blaring out of Scott's Jeep.

"Meyer, let me see that thing," beckons Gee.

"Well I don't really have a choice, do I, Gee. It is on my face. Oh, you decided to go with the handlebar to start the month. Very nice."

Rado and Jack continue to shoot.

"Yup, I figure midmonth I'll take the bars off and ride straight up, but until then I'll be stroking this baby all day."

"You look good. Happy Mustache May."

Gee bows at his rounded waist.

"Thank you, and a happy Mustache May to you as well."

"Will you fags get over and get ready to hoop."

"Hey, Rado, just 'cause that peach fuzz don't come in like you want it to doesn't mean you gotta sass me and Gee."

"I try and I try. If my dad could've given me one thing of his in a hereditary line, one would think it would be the ability to grow a stache. But no, I get to be skinny and short."

Rado shoots and the ball rims off into my hands. I venture out to the three-point line.

"It's good to see you're continuing with the Asian stache, Jacky."

"I'm doing what I can do. I'm glad I can't grow shit like you though, Meyer. How do you even go out in public without getting arrested for that molester shit?"

I lob an errant shot. "That's the key, no public inter-action. I can't even make eye contact with people without getting the cops called on me. It's just good I don't live next to an elementary school. Hey, why do we have to play ball at an elementary school?"

"What are you going to do about your accounts?"

"You ski, Rado, you know how it works. The stache is so off the charts right now that my accounts will just think that I'm unique in an ever-growing blob of indi-viduality that all somehow looks the same. You know how many assholes I see wearing classic Ray-Bans at events now, trying to stand out, when all five of their long-haired buddies are wearing the same thing? It's sad. The day I see someone in the industry wearing

JNCOs will be the day I see a true individual, and I will shake his hand."

I hoist another shot that hits back rim and the rebound bounces toward Wilson's Nissan pulling into the parking lot.

"God, when were JNCOs cool again? Like, seventh grade?"

"The baggier the better, my friend."

"I could fit my girlfriend in mine."

"I bet you guys fucked all day at recess, didn't you, Jacky."

"My dick was as small as it is now, so it's not like that was taking up any extra room in there."

We all stop shooting and look at Jack for some signal that he's joking, but he gives nothing because if he doesn't he knows we'll believe him. Jack's done some messed-up stuff that I know is true, so I put nothing by him now.

"Mariners up seven to five in the eighth. Hardgrove is bringing in Putz early," Scotty informs us from a leaning position against his Jeep.

Wilson emerges from his car looking as big as ever. He recently moved to Seattle from Spokane (upgrade) for a new job. Still, he's studying for this CFA accreditation exam and has been spending minimal time with friends because of this test, so the fact he's playing ball today is big news. I head his direction.

"Jeffrey. Good to see you out of the cave."

"I figured I could take one afternoon off for some basketball."

"That's nice to hear. How is the studying coming?"

Wilson looks sideways in obvious distaste at the thought of this test. I feel bad for bringing it up, but that's about the only thing we have to talk about these days. Scotty heads back to the court. Putz must have got out of the jam.

"I don't know, man. I think I know this stuff, but we'll see."

"You'll do fine. You wouldn't let yourself do poorly. Come on, get some shots in before we run."

We turn back to the court where the four others have started a lay-up line.

"Where's Shoe and Dan?"

"On their way."

"One other thing."

"Yeah?"

"You got something on your face, dude."

Jeff has a high giggle for someone his size.

"Fuck off."

FEBRUARY 22ND / 2006 / SEATTLE

Because my bedroom window is open the street noise on Stone is louder than usual. J-Bird's over. We watched a movie earlier and just finished having sex. I have to open the store tomorrow morning. J-Bird's rolled away from me, facing the wall. It's weird sleeping in the same bed with someone again.

"What are we? I mean, what are we doing?"

Shit. Talk time.

"Huh?"

"Is this going to go anywhere, Jon, or are we just fucking?"

"No, no. You know I like hanging out with you, it's just when I moved to Seattle I didn't want to date anyone for a while. I've told you this. We're still getting to know each other."

Not bad. So tired. I can't believe this is happening right now.

"Well...you know... we've been spending a lot of time together the last month or so, and I just wanted to know how you felt because I think I'm starting to really like you."

"I like you too."

"C'mon, Jon, if you're just fucking me and don't want this to go anywhere, please tell me now so I can move on."

Pause. Say the right thing. You know what you want. I hate these fucking talks.

"J-Bird, I really do like you. I think that's obvious. There's an attraction here that I can't really explain yet."

I roll over and slide my right arm underneath her neck, and pull myself behind her.

"Can I call you my girlfriend?" I kiss her on the cheek and feel her face smile.

We make love for the first time as a couple.

"Hey, Breezy, this Jon...the Helly rep. Um, the guy who sold you that jacket. You must be in class. Anyways, it's a nice day outside and I was wondering if you wanted to hit some golf balls? You know, I just don't think we should be running around and sweating and stuff on our first date. Well, it's not even a date, more of a hang out. So...yeah, well, give me a call back so we can set something up. All right, I guess I'll talk to you later."

Nice. She's not freaked out or anything after that.

I'm comfortably watching PTI when I hear my phone start to vibrate behind me on the kitchen counter stool. My shirtless back unsticks from the chair when I stand up. The afternoon sun is penetrating the apartment, creating a nasty glare on the TV. I get to the phone as my ringer starts. Holy shit. It's her.

"Breezy, how ya doing?"

"I'm all right, I'm all right. What are you up to?"

Don't say anything that makes you sound like a slacker.

"Um, just researching some accounts out of the home office. You?"

"Well I just got done with class, and am free the rest of the afternoon. You want to do something?"

"Yeah, did you listen to my message?"

"No."

Thank fucking God.

"Oh no reason, I just thought we might go hit some range balls instead of tennis. A little easier on the body, you know?"

"Sure, how 'bout you give me thirty minutes."

"Yeah, sounds...fantastic. I'll pick you up then?"

"Sure, you know that Shell station on Nickerson?"

"Yeah."

"Take a left and the first building on the left is mine."

"OK, thirty minutes."

"See ya."

"See ya."

I take the left at the Shell station, and pull up in front of what looks like an off-campus apartment complex for SPU upperclassmen. Huh, must be a junior. I get out of the Element to make sure I'll be able to open the door for her. I take my phone out of my cargo shorts pocket and call Breezy, but before I get a ring tone she pops out the building door. She looks amazing. Tan legs bounding out of a jean miniskirt, cute little white baseball tee, and ragged converse sneakers with no laces. And the smile. Incredible.

"You're on top of things."

"I like your car."

"Thanks, it's pretty nice when it's not in the shop."

I open the passenger side door and make sure she gets in without incident, and of course to come off as a gentleman. I left the music on pretty loud. Shit. The first thing I do when I get in is turn the Weezer down. I figured it was good, safe choice; a respected band that gives off the impression of an intelligent alternative state of mind.

"What's this?"

She's found the kicker to the date that I'm hoping will go over well.

"I had some leftover cards from when I was writing thank-you notes to accounts, so I thought I'd give you one."

Breezy smiles and opens the envelope with her name on the front in my scratchy, slightly angled handwriting. She's smiling. Good.

On the inside of the card I wrote, "Thanks for the great date."

"I like it. Thank you."

"Now we just gotta make it happen."

I pull into Interbay's parking lot. Conversation is going well. Her mom wanted her to go to Gonzaga. She didn't like SPU at first but now it's all right. She's only been golfing with her grandpa and it sucked. These are all good things.

After unloading from the Element with my set of golf clubs and Breezy, I grab the pro shop door. A group of after-work suits have shed their blazers and are practicing their putting on the adjacent green. This place has to make bank.

I purchase a large bucket while pushing away Breezy's cash.

"Next time I'll get it," she says.

"So there's already going to be a next time?"

"Sure."

I turn back to the attendant with what has to be a smug smirk, and take our tokens. We head up to the second deck because there are always fewer people up there. She'll be more comfortable.

"Are you going to teach me something today?"

"Yeah, but I'm going to keep it clean."

"What do you mean?"

"I'm not going to do the dirty Zach Morris move and slide up from behind while wrapping my arms you, whispering in your ear to grip the club lighter. You can't even swing with someone doing that."

"It is the first date."

"Exactly, no need to get uncomfortable, at least till the end of the bucket so I at least get my money's worth."

Being a nice day, most of the hitting stalls are occupied with work-cheating golf hobbyists. There's a break of about ten spots toward the end of the row. I get our range balls from the machine, and we move to the open spaces. I pour the range balls evenly into adjacent hitting stations. I take the mat on the right so I'm not standing behind Breezy constantly looking at her ass, which would be blatantly obvious and she would definitely notice.

"All right, ready to go?"

"You know what you're doing, don't you?"

"Um, yeah, maybe."

I grab for a nine iron for Breezy. I take out the two iron for myself and start to stretch. The sun breaks on the roof, hitting only our legs.

"OK, so grab the club at both ends, and rotate your arms in front of you. Stretching is very important."

"If you say so."

She does as I say and twists her arms until they're crossed in front of her.

"I think this stretch is harder than hitting a ball. Where'd you learn this?"

"From an assistant UW coach years ago. It was some clinic for the best and the brightest young golfers of Eastern Washington. More of a recruiting trip, I think now."

"So you didn't make it, huh? Never got a call from the U?"

"Nope, the UW roster was filled when I went calling, so I was happy when Gonzaga decided to have me." I nod to my old blue team bag with, "Gonzaga University" down the right side, and "Jonathan Meyer, Ellensburg, WA" stitched into the small pocket. One of my most prized possessions.

"Oh, so were you going to tell me this?"

I kick off my sandals, step onto the mat, and hit my first ball.

"I was going to wait for you to ask. I figured for a first date I should try to impress you as much as possible because after this it's all downhill," I hit another ball

and turn back to her. She's shaking her head while setting up for a shot.

"OK, let's take a look at your grip here." I move to
the barrier separating our stations, and squat down
taking hold of her hands that are holding the grip of
the nine iron.

"Looks pretty good, Breezy. Your grandpa did a
nice job for what time he had with his bitter grand-
daughter."

I lightly touch her right hand until it's in a neutral
position, and move her right pinky into the crevasse
located between her left index and middle finger.

"There you go, the overlapping grip. Best grip in the
game."

"My grandpa said to use the interlocking grip,"
Breezy chirps jokingly. I release her soft hands, look up
at her and smile.

"Is your grandpa here now? That grip will give you
blisters all day. OK, set up to the ball."

Breezy approaches the ball, rocking on her heels.
All in all, she's exercising nice angles.

"All right, the only swing tip I'm going to give you
today is...well two tips...OK first tip. Throughout your
backswing keep the left arm straight at all times. Second, I want you to focus on the furthest dimple forward
on the golf ball. Where your eyes look the club will
hit, and the best shots are when the ball is hit before
the ground on a downswing. Was that too much to
take in?"

"Nope, I think I got it."

I back away into my station. Breezy takes a wonderful, fundamental swing, and the ball pops into the air. After the ball lands we look back at each other. Her eyes are wide and she's smiling that beautiful smile; the smile of someone who has just accomplished something they didn't think they could do.

"I think you're going to be all right, Breezy. That will be fifty dollars for Dr. Meyer."

"Shut up and hit your balls," she mutters with a smile.

"Fair enough." I turn back to my trough of black and white balls. "That's the only advice you're getting today then with an attitude like that."

I do as she says and start swinging six irons. From time to time I hear a break in her hitting balls, aware of her watching me. I'm just trying not to shank.

"So, Breezy, what are we doing for a major?"

"Pardon?"

"Your major, what you're going to school for?"

"Oh, um, I haven't declared one yet."

"What do you mean, aren't you a junior or senior?"

"No, I'm a sophomore."

"Oh."

"I'm nineteen."

My brow furrows. "Wow."

That's interesting. Fuck. Holy shit. Fuck. She's only nineteen. Holy shit. What are you doing? You're twenty-four. She's so young. But you didn't know that. She's so hot. Of course she's hot, she's only nineteen. Too much of an age difference even for *The Theory*. She's so tan.

"Jon?"

"Huh, oh sorry."

"You were just staring at my legs for like, five seconds."

"Um, sorry. Just doing some math."

"Meyer, please don't come over here and bitch to me about going out with a nineteen-year-old—OK? If she would have said that to me I instantly would have jumped over the barrier and tried to have sex with her. Issue? There is no issue here."

Jack takes a drag of his cigarette, leans back over the banister of his Lower Queen Anne, third-floor apartment's porch, and looks out over Elliot Bay. I'm sitting in a patio chair next to the barbeque. The sun beats down on us.

"Jacky, I think nineteen is too young even for *The Theory.*"

"This fucking 'theory' of yours is going to keep you from sweet pieces of ass. What's the problem? You're single now. What difference does age make as long as it's legal?"

"It's the maturity level Jacky, which is really throwing me for a loop because she's totally cool. I just can't believe it. And what—am I going to hook up with her in her dorm room? How fucking cool is it to have sex on a college stock twin bed? I'm done with that shit. I was done with that after sophomore year."

"Well, she's not done with that 'cause she's still a sophomore."

The apartment door inside opens and shuts. Rado comes into view and joins us on the deck.

"Sup, Rado?"

"Hey boys, how's it hanging?"

"Well, Meyer here has problems that every other man in the world would trade him for."

R.J. lights up a heater.

"Tell him."

Rado takes his first drag as I look up from my seated position.

"I just went on a great date with a chick that I thought was like, twenty-three when I asked her out, but came to find out she's nineteen."

"Huh. She's hot, right?"

"The hottest girl I've ever taken out. Seems cool."

"So what's the problem?"

"Yeah, Jon, what is the problem? Why don't you explain your little theory to R.J. here?"

"OK, so *The Theory* developed when I was working at the Helly store. One of my co-workers, a girl our age, was dating like a thirty-six-year-old asshole, but I thought it was OK because even with the age difference, they had the same maturity level. I mean, this guy was a loser, harping on her all the time, sometimes in the store. So *The Theory* goes: As long as maturity levels are equal, age does not matter. The problem now is do I heed my own advice."

"So this chick is pretty cool, then. Not ditsy or anything."

"Totally cool. No high, squeaky sorority voice. Worldly. She's taking a lot of global event-type classes, and is waiting to hear back about whether she got into the SPU graphic design program, which I guess is a fairly big deal."

"And she's hot?"

I look directly at Rado to emphasize my point.

"The best legs I've ever seen. I'm fucked, man."

Jacky drags on his cig and takes it away from his mouth, still looking over the bay.

"Meyer, I'm going to punch you in the face if you don't pursue this thing, if not for you, for me. I need this, man. I need to know there's hope out there."

"Go easy, Jacky."

"Do you realize when we were seniors in college, your little nineteen-year-old was finishing up her senior year of high school?"

"God, you're right."

Laughing, "That's awesome. Does she know you're twenty-four?"

"Yeah, I talked about being out of school, the *Real World*, that sort of stuff. She didn't seem to care."

Both nod. Jack's cigarette is roached out. Rado is taking longer and longer drags, trying to catch up. Must have been a long day in the office. The sun starts setting behind the Olympics. Nice night for a Mariners game.

"Well Meyer...(drag)...keep us updated on the situation. You know we got nothing better going on with our relationships. Something fresh like this in someone else's life is just what I need."

"Will do Rado."

I stand up from my patio chair. Sigh deeply.

"All right, I'm out of here. Thanks for the support guys. Heading to Alki if either of you are interested. Swan's hosting a night of beer pong."

"I think we're doing Ozzie's tonight."

"Ozzie's again, huh? OK, well if you change your mind just call. Swan's is easy to find. Right on the beach."

Jack informs me, "That's no beach, Meyer."

"Well, it's something for those of us not from LA."

I slide back into the apartment through the torn insect screen, climb the three steps out of the sunken living room, and open the door to leave.

"Don't fuck this up for us, Meyer!"

I couldn't agree more.

Don't fuck this up. Don't fuck this up.

"Hey, Breezy, I got your text and yeah, uh, I thought things today went really well too, and I was just checking in to see if you might be coming down this direction. You can text again or call, it doesn't matter. Well, it's pretty loud so you should just probably text. We're just playing some beer pong down here, Alki that is. Swan and I—you don't know him, he's the best—well, we've been killing it and have won like five games, HEY SWAN! HOW MANY GAMES HAVE WE WON? FIVE! YEAH, OK, SEE YA IN A SECOND! NO! YOU DON'T KNOW

HER! HAHA I KNOW, MAN. I'M TRYING TO GET HER HERE! Anyways, we're having a really good time and I wish you were here. God, it's really dark outside."

"Sorry, I mean, today was so cool and you're into art and photography and stuff like that. I just love that 'cause that's what I'm into, and having things in common rocks. I really do want to see some of your work. OK, this is getting a little long. Does your phone have the option for me to start this thing over? Whatever. Talk to you soon I hope...Breezy."

I hate these Goddamn boxes. So much product. I guess it's better than having to stand at the front of the store.

"So, Mary, what's up with you and Joe lately?"

"Same old thing. Playing video games with his buddies. It's not even worth fighting about anymore. You and J-Bird all right?"

"Uh, same old thing. Just on cruise control. Her birthday is coming up. I think I'm going to take her to the coast."

"That's sounds like fun. She'll like that."

"I think so too. I haven't been over there before. Maybe we'll surf?"

That last statement even surprises me. Mary looks good today. I grab more stickers from the bottom a new box, and start stickering the next batch of fleeces. Mindless. Lyndsay emerges from the back with a smile on her face. She's excited about something, moving quickly.

"Jon! Jon. I was just talking to Mel and she said the So Cal rep position is open, and that Goodie isn't working for Debi anymore. The Northwest junior rep position is open too. You should totally talk to her about it. You'd be perfect."

Huh. Wonder what happened? I could work for Debi. She seems all right. Never too crazy all those times I've modeled for her when at corporate.

"All right, calm down, Lyndz. Who says that I want to leave the store? I mean I'm pretty happy here making $9.75 an hour, barely scraping by with my degree from Gonzaga."

"Right, I forgot. We're all so happy to be working here. You gotta pursue this thing, Jon. Give others inspiration that there's life outside of retail."

Although we're joking, she's right. This place, this box of clothes has to go. Can't grow in here. Arrested Development.

"Lyndz, I'm loving it. OK, next time I'm at corporate I'll talk to Ric. See what he thinks."

"Must be nice to have the ear of the CEO?"

"Has its advantages."

"Time to call in one more favor."

"Once again, Lyndz, I think you're right."

"Am I ever wrong?"

"Remember freshman year when you failed that English test? You were wrong then."

"You failed that test too."

"We're not talking about me and I didn't spend that night hanging out of my bed, puking into a trash can out of spite for the professor."

"No, you just tried to have sex with her."

"Not true! Just wanted to. That's a low blow Lyndz. Anyways, puking never raised anyone's grade, and she looked good for her age."

MAY 5ᵀᴴ / 2007 / SEATTLE

You're a fucking jerk. I can't believe you're doing this. Make the call. I push the talk button on my humongous BlackBerry. Why did I get this phone again?

"Hello?"

"Hey, A-bomb…"

"Yeah,"

"This is Jon. Jon Meyer."

"Wow. Jon…how are you? I mean, it's been awhile."

"Well, yeah. I'm good. I'm good. I know it's late but me and some friends are heading to the Pac Inn and I wondered if you wanted to come.

A-bomb measures her reply.

"Um, yeah…I'm not doing anything."

"Sure. Are you still living by Lake Union?"

"No, no. We're up on Seventy-third near Phinney. You know it?"

"Of course. I'll be there in ten."

"OK, see you then."

I hang up and grab my fleece. Everyone is starting to move. The apartment is destroyed. Multitudes of empty beer cans rest on the Ping-Pong table from round after round of flip cup. The destruction continues to the coffee table where the girls were sitting. Who were those girls? They didn't go to Gonzaga.

"Where you going, Meyer?"

"To pick up an old friend."

I shouldn't be driving. I haven't driven in this bad a condition since college, and someone was always with me then to double-check decisions. Traffic is light. Street lamps highlight the large trees that are hanging over the neighborhood with an orange glow. I stop in front of the only house on the block with an inside light on. I push the talk button twice. Before I can put the phone to my ear, A-bomb walks in front of the living room window, and seconds later opens the front door. She hops down the stairs in designer-looking jeans and a pea coat. Her dark, shimmering hair is pulled back into a ponytail. Half heels give her a few added inches. I didn't give her a lot of time to get ready, but she did fine. She pulls on the passenger door handle, but I've forgotten to unlock the door.

"Sorry!"

Clumsily, I push the automatic lock button and A-bomb bounces into the Element.

"Hey."

"Hey, how are you?"

"Fine. I'm glad you called. I was just watching TV."

"Oh, well, that's no fun."

"I have to work tomorrow."

I pull away from the curb, accelerating through parked cars on both sides of the street.

"We won't keep you out too late, then."

"It's your call."

"One beer?"

"Maybe one water."

"Oh, you can tell."

"I can smell."

"We were playing flip cup. I was captain. My team needed me to show up."

"And did you?"

"Sometimes...we weren't very good. The middle of the table was awful. My fault though, I picked the team. Lack of chemistry, ya know?"

I take a turnabout a little too fast, and the Element sways. A-bomb looks a little nervous.

We blow through the door into the Pacific Inn where the rest of the party has posted up at a couple of booths. I'm not going to put her through socializing with them. Regulars mind their drinks at the bar top. The back room has a pool table, but is otherwise empty. It's darker in here than the night outside. We sit down on a walnut bench that matches the walls.

"So what's the occasion?"

"A couple of us had birthdays in April, so this is kind of a group b-day thing."

"Ah, those group b-day things."

"You know 'em?"

"All too well."

Where do we go from here? You do need a water.

"Hey, I'm going to get a water. You want one?"

"Sure."

Back in the main room, inquisitive looks and winks from the gallery come from every booth. This one is mine and they don't get to know her. No ties. No name to pass forward and gossip about. The bartender is kind enough to adhere my request of two waters. I wink back to my observing patrons, and return to A-bomb. She's in the same position; her small frame taking up minimal space. She accepts the water from me with two hands, cupping it into her body so she doesn't spill. I fall back on the bench.

"So what have you been up to? It's been awhile."

"I've been working just like every other grad. The pizza world is as boring as ever. They still haven't moved me up to corporate."

"For accounting, right?"

"Very good."

"Well, you're just probably so valuable in the store that they can't let you go."

A-bomb turns her head in shy acceptance and takes a drink of water. The rim of the pint glass magnifies the mole above her lip.

"I'm sure that's it. And you, Mr. Meyer...has life been good to you?"

I take a gulp of water.

"Can't complain. I'm on salary and do nothing all day. I look for things to do, but it never gets anywhere. I'm in one of those funks where even though I have all the time in the world to do something, I can't muster the energy to accomplish it because I've been doing jack for so long. What do they say...with copious amounts of free time comes great responsibility?"

"I don't think anyone says that."

 I accept this critiscm.

"Want to get out of here before things get wild?"

"Yes."

 I crawl into A-bomb's bed, boxers only, still drunk. The ceiling isn't swirling yet. That's nice. A-bomb's brushing her teeth. The noticeable buzzing of a Sonicare resonates from the bathroom. I wish I could brush my teeth. My mouth tastes like cheap beer. Clean and dirty laundry litters the floor of her room. She's already apologized for the mess. Her bed is comfortable. Great pillows.

A-bomb re-enters and turns the light off. She's in gray UW sweats and a tank top. She says something but it doesn't register, and burrows under the flower print down comforter. I slide my right arm under her neck and she rolls the backside of her body into me. I begin kissing her neck, wasting no time, and catch a glimpse of her soft breasts meshing together. My left hand begins on her thigh, and moves until it's clutching her left breast. She's starting to pant. That was easy. My left hand makes another move for her sweatpant's hem while my mouth continues on her neck, lightly kissing as to not leave any unwanted marks. Who knows, maybe she wants a hickey? I lightly touch and stroke around her. My wrist is met by her hand and is pulled back up to her waist. She says something about bad timing. Fuck. More like no fuck. Whatever. I push myself up with my right elbow, and begin kissing A-bomb's lips. They're soft, which isn't surprising. She takes care of herself.

I'm hard by the time A-bomb moves to the top position. My head sinks into a pillow. We French lightly, tongues barely touching. Her hands frame my face. They never move below my neck.

I notice glow stars in the corner of her room. Why are you kissing with your eyes open? I ask A-bomb about the glow stars, and it amuses her. She burrows her face in my neck.

Running from the Cog, I'm late for American history on only the second day of the class. If only Professor Hughes didn't let us eat in class, I wouldn't be running to the cafeteria trying to grab some sustenance so I can make it through lecture without falling asleep. I take every other stair into the Ad Building, crank the door, and steps later settle into the only desk left front and center.

"So you nice of you join us Mister?"

"Meyer. Jon Meyer."

Hughes asks, "And, Mr. Meyer, what do you think of the designated hitter?" Then turns around, awaiting my argument.

Fuck, I just sat down. I heard he was like this. Likes to talk about random shit every day. His beard is starting to turn white. He's leaning down to hear my answer, which takes away more height than he has to give. Glasses he hasn't replaced from the seventies are framing smoky eyes that are currently piercing my soul. Gather yourself.

"I'm in favor of it, Professor Hughes. I believe that it gives veterans like Edgar Martinez a chance to extend their careers, and who wants to see pitchers hit anyways? If they don't strike out they just bunt runners over. I believe the DH has been good for the game of baseball."

That gets a few nods from the class. Nice.

Hughes snaps back around on point. "Wrong answer, my friend! I'm a Dodgers fan and therefore a National League fan. The DH has disgraced the game and should be taken out of professional baseball."

We're off to a nice start. Hughes launches off on some rant about the DH, eventually tying it in with the JFK assassination. I crack the bag of chips from the Cog and start munching away. I'm starving, and without calories or something to occupy my mind my chin will start hitting my chest in ten minutes. I'm trying to eat these chips as quietly as possible, but I don't think it's working.

"And, Mr. Meyer, if you could refrain from...well... chewing, I think that would make the class go much smoother."

Mouth full of Ghardettos, I bow in humiliation. Two for Hughes. Zero for Meyer.

I exit stage right after surviving the rest of class sans humiliation. Hughes decided to take pity on me after properly searing me in the early minutes. I need a nap. I wonder if Matt's back in the room? I should probably learn his schedule.

A cute blonde with a small nose bounces up alongside me.

"Hey, I'm Angie."

"Um, hi, Angie, I'm Jon."

"I know, I was just in American history with you."

"Right, is it too late to transfer?"

"I think he likes you."

"Well, if he wants to talk baseball we can do that during office hours. My main focus in that class is to get some food down, in turn absorbing knowledge with calories."

Angie smiles and it's a good smile. Feeling better, I return the smile. She's still tan from what looks like a summer spent in the sun. She's wearing jeans and a petit T-shirt. Small breasts give the shirt a light tug, pulling it just above the top of her jeans, teasing what has to be a beautiful stomach. I avert my eyes back to hers, trying to minimize the scope.

"Maybe next class avoid the Ghardettos. The little brown guys will get you every time."

"You could hear it too?"

"Oh yeah, all the way in the back."

"Maybe I should just sit in the back next time?"

"I think that's a good idea."

We come to the fork in hallway. I thumb left. Angie thumbs right. We square to one another.

"This is how it ends?"

"Guess so."

"See you on Thursday."

"See you on Thursday."

I bound down the cracked stairs of the Admin Building, into the fresh fall sun. Swan and Scheibel are working on a crossword puzzle outside of Crosby. Scheibel's muttonchops grew out nicely over the summer. Swan, however, looks the same. Standard issue shorts, sandals, and T-shirt complementing short hair and a stubbled beard. The sunny day has brought what looks like half of the student population to the quad. College activities are taking place: Frisbee, blanket reading, and flirting.

"Hey, guys."

"Meyer, what's up, man? Care to join the fight?"

"I've never been able to do those things."

I collapse onto Crosby's steps.

"How are classes going for you two so far?"

"Just stuck in the business building. Swan's got Munroe in a couple of classes."

"Really, I'm about to check up on him right now in CM."

"Wait, did you just say CM?"

"As in the freshman dorm? Yes, I thought I told you guys we got stuck there. Not everyone can squat in The Hotel. We got fucked on our lottery number. First choice on rooms though. If you guys ever want to go come over and check out the freshmen talent all you have to do is ask."

Swan and Scheibel look at each other.

"How 'bout now?"

"Let's do it."

We stroll through the quad, intercepting Frisbee passes and commenting on every girl that comes into sight. I don't feel tired anymore. I love the first month of school. We're sophomores. We're the kings of on-campus living.

I unlock the outside door to the northwest wing. The boys live on the bottom floor of CM while the ladies occupy the top. For supposedly being lighter on their feet, the chicks above us have been making plenty of noise.

"Welcome back to CM, gentlemen."

Looking about, Swan admits, "I never thought I'd be back in this place again, at least with two guys."

"That's right, Swan, you hooked up with Sasha a couple of times last year, didn't you? You know she's back in here, right? Has her own single."

"That's all you, Meyer. Whew, that chick was a freak."

"Well, she's on the opposite side of the building. Too far of a walk for me. Here we are."

I unlock my door and walk into a darkened room. The only light is coming from Matt's computer screen, reflecting off his face. What's he...shit.

"GET OUT! GET THE FUCK OUT!"

I look closer at the monitor and see two women acting in non-catholic practices.

"Oops, sorry, Matty. Is this a new one?"

He looks directly at me.

"MEYER! GET THE FUCK OUT!"

"Sorry, sorry."

I ease back out of the room to find Swan and Scheibel on the hallway floor laughing hysterically. I lean against the door and slide down, a smile beginning on my face. Soon enough, I'm rolling with them in hysteria.

From behind the door comes a muffled voice.

"You guys are dicks. I can't even finish now."

Scheibel inquires whether we can come in. After a few beats the door opens, and I fall into the room. Matt stands above me, his pointed finger quick to move to the others.

"Assholes. Each and every one of you."

I'm watching Sunday golf, stroking the stache, waiting to fall asleep. My phone vibrates. Reply text from J-Bird.

"No. Don't you think that would put a strain on the friendship?"

"Maybe. I just know it will feel good."

I set the phone on the arm of the chair in case of a return message.

Vibration.

"I'm not saying it wouldn't. It just has to happen naturally."

"Like when we're watching a movie together?"

Vibration.

"Yes, something like that."

"Or out in the woods?"

Vibration.

"That would work too."

"Understood. Want to watch a movie?"

Vibration.
"*You're hopeless.*"
"*Hopelessly horny.*"

Vibration.
"*If I didn't know you, I'd think you were a bigger ass-hole than I already think you are.*"
"*Thanks, that means a lot coming from you.*"

Vibration.
"*You're welcome.*"

It's nice outside so I decide to walk. The trees on Stone are casting needed shadows over the sidewalk. I can't believe she found me on MySpace. This is weird. I cross Stone and head up Fortieth. Shelter is once again found under the trees. I'm starting to sweat under my short-sleeve button-up. That's no good. My feet hurt. I need new sandals. Not too much longer until the café.

There's a nice five-bedroom, three-bath cottage-style home with a lovely garden house for sale past Wallingford Ave. I'm observing flowers when I hear steps coming from down the sidewalk.

"Hey, what are you doing up here? The café is four blocks back the other way."

"I need the exercise."

"Fair enough. Let's get some coffee."

A-bomb looks great, which isn't a good thing. Her olive skin has taken to the early summer sun. She needs to look bad to make this easier. We start walking back to the café.

"So, how's life? You were at UW, right?"

"Yup, all finished up. Can't say I'm really putting the degree to use yet."

"What do you mean?"

"I'm still at Pagliaccis making pizzas, or telling people how to make pizzas."

"Hey, anything to pay the bills, or in our case, college loans."

A-bomb shakes her head. "You'd just think that with a degree you'd be doing something better, ya know?"

"I don't really know anyone who's doing what they really want right now. Don't worry about it, A-bomb."

"You're not doing what you want?"

Wow.

"Working retail and valeting three nights a week? Can't say I'm exactly living the dream quite yet."

"You'd rather be doing valet full time?"

"Very funny, but no."

Stop being funny.

"I'm still holding out for that National Geographic assignment to fall into my lap."

We take our seats in the deep, wood-framed patio chairs outside the café. A-bomb advised me against hot coffee due to the weather, so I'm drinking an iced mocha. She's sipping on a frappucino-type concoction. Small talk time.

"So is there a boyfriend in A-bomb's life?"

Boring start.

"Nope, not in a while. The house I lived in sophomore year had four girls dating four guys from another house, but since then...nothing. You?"

"Boyfriend? No, well more of a BFF situation, but he lives in California. Girlfriend? Yes. Been together for around seven months now. She's in Mexico for two weeks. She's in the nursing program at the U. We just got…she just got a dog. We think she's a lab-collie mix. But you knew that already, didn't you?"

"What? That you just got a dog?"

"No, that I have a girlfriend."

"Oh, yeah, well I can read. MySpace *is* great for stalking."

"Well, I'm happy you found me. It was very unexpected. God, was it two summers ago that Justin lived with you?"

"Yup, how is Justin?"

"He's actually down in Vegas selling real estate. Doing really well. I saw him last March. Still looks the same."

"Messy thin hair and expensive-looking clothes?"

"You bet."

"Some people never change."

"You can say that again."

MAY 11TH / 2007 / SEATTLE

The Physiofit is resting in its usual spot at the end of the bike rack. I fumble with my keys until I finally find the one for the bike lock, and wrench the steel slinky from the rack. It was the cheapest lock available, and if I had spent any more, the lock would've ended up costing me more than the bike. I hop on the extra-large seat. Shit, the tires are going flat again. I push the "open" button for the garage door, and loop around the parking garage until the door is fully up. With momentum I make it halfway up Stone without having to change gears. Rarely do I utilize all ten gears the Physiofit has to offer. For forty dollars, I really have gotten my money's worth out of this bike. I guess it could be defined as a hybrid, but not your usual mountain/road bike combo. The Physiofit offers a beautiful blue mountain bike frame, but with beach cruiser handlebars. I have yet to see another like it in Seattle.

The two tennis rackets in my backpack are starting to pull the zipper down, wanting to escape. I hope Angie finds the courts. I really don't want to have to sit around and wait for her.

I cross Forty-fifth, and then take side streets the rest of the way to the Lower Woodlands courts. The nice day has brought out the usual characters along with a few newbies I don't recognize. The old guys are taking up four courts, playing their daily doubles matches. I love it.

Angie and her car are nowhere to be seen. No surprise. I lean my bike up against the Gatorade machine and walk onto one of the available courts. In the adjacent court, the Asian woman who's here as often as me is giving a lesson to a rich-looking white lady. I pull my random, flat tennis balls out of my backpack, and start taking some easy serves. The Asian coach is obviously annoyed that I'm taking the other court. Just wait till Angie gets here. My right arm is still a little tight from hitting with A-bomb the other day.

Angie's white Oldsmobile Aurora creeps past the court, and then crackles into the parking spot next to the white lady's Mercedes. Angie pops out wearing skimpy black shorts and a tangerine tank top. She looks good. Still tan from her trip to Hawaii.

"Hey, girl."

"What's up, playboy?"

"Nothing, just glad you made it. Taking off a day of work for 'Angie time'? I like it."

"Yup, wanted to see what your relaxed life is like. I have to run some errands after this too…trip stuff."

"It is a life of leisure. Three weeks, right?"

"End of the month. Speaking of months, your stache still looks disgusting."

Angie is not a fan of Mustache May.

"Please shave that thing, Jon. You're a good-looking guy, and this is not adding to your physical value."

"Angie, I don't have a choice. Now are you ready to get a tennis lesson or what?"

"I don't know, you seem pretty intense."

"Well do you want to get better?"

"I guess."

"OK, then, let's just start bouncing the ball in the air. This is going to work on our hand-eye coordination."

I hand Angie the extra racket, and she starts popping the ball in the air sporadically, having to chase down the ball after every unsuccessful bounce. This could be bad. She catches me laughing.

"Jon, you can't laugh. If you laugh I'm leaving."

"Sorry, sorry. It's just, you're an athletic person. I have confidence in your abilities. Let's start hitting and see how that goes."

I collect our balls from around the court that I had been serving. The Asian coach has a full on glare at me. My coaching techniques aren't at her level, yet.

"All right, Angie, get it back to me."

I pull a ball from my shorts pocket and hit it over the net. Angie watches the ball, pulls the racket back, and nothing. She swings and misses, and swings and misses at every ball I hit at her, for thirty minutes.

"Sorry I'm embarrassing you in front of your tennis friends."

"I think that's enough for today. Bring it in, student. At least you look good, and really, that's all that's important."

"Thanks. What are you up to tonight?"

"Nothing."

"Lyndz is coming over for dinner. You want to come?"
"For sure. What time?"
"Seven."
"Cool, I'll be there."

I showered after tennis so there's no need for another. It's still warm so I put on cargo shorts and one of my Smith tees. I snipe a hoodie for good measure. Should I walk? If there was ever a night. I decide against it, grab my car keys, and drive the short distance to the girls' place past Phinney.

Not surprisingly, Lyndsay is running late, but that hasn't stopped Angie from starting dinner. Ashley and Liz are out for the night man-hunting. Ideally, later on they'll bring some poor soul home for dissection. Their track record hasn't been too good lately.

"So what's for dinner, baby girl?"
"Veggie pizza with mushrooms and peppers."

Angie's a vegetarian, but is trying to eat meat again because of her trip to South America coming up. It's not going well so far, as apparent by the menu tonight.

"Sounds delish. Lyndz running late?"
"Yeah, she and Evan are fighting. She can't get off the phone."
"So how do you know that?"
"She took my call and then went back to Evan's."
"Nice."

Angie's wearing jeans, which is a change from her standard home wear of sweat pants. However, she is sporting one of Andrea's hoodies to bring the balance back. She's cupping a glass of red wine while sprinkling the mushrooms on the pizza.

"You like mushrooms?"

 No.

"Sure, they're fine."

"Well speak up now or deal with it later."

"I guess I'll deal."

"OK, sour pants."

"How was the rest of the day?"

"Got my immunizations done so that was fun. Picked up some malaria pills. Time for the nightmares."

"You know, I never had nightmares when I had to take mine for Panama."

"Lucky guy."

"Clear conscious."

"Maybe."

 Angie hands me a goblet and I fill it with some six-dollar merlot. I hate it when red wine stains your teeth. I wonder how many glasses you have to drink before that happens? Lyndz pops in the front door.

"Helloooo!"

"Hey, Lyndz."

"Hey, Jon. Didn't know you were coming over."

"You betcha."

"So what's for dinner?"

"Veggie pizza."

"Angie, I thought we were going to do a meat dish?"

"I'm sorry but I can't. I'm just not ready yet."

"What are you going to do in Peru when people are offering you some meat that they slaughtered just for you? Say, 'sorry, I've got a veggie pizza in the oven'?"

"Maybe."

"Hopeless."

We eat. I can't taste the mushrooms, thank God, and finish my second large piece of pizza. The food is offsetting the glasses of wine, keeping my intoxication at a buzz. The three of us have moved to the living room, and have landed upon one of our more popular topics like what are we going to do with our lives. Lyndsay's just started at Nordstrom and is making killer money. At least double what she was making at Helly.

"So you like it though?"

"Yeah, it's all right. I'm busier during the day than al Helly, at least more consistent."

"But no more cheap jackets. How are you ever going to stay warm in the winter?"

"Well, that's where you come in, Jon. How is repping going?"

"Uh, fine. I'm just so bored. I honestly try to find things to do during the day, but that ends after a couple of phone calls. I'm going to Oregon twice over the next couple of weeks for some rail jam comps, so that will be nice to get out Seattle for a couple of days. My brother is going to be in Ellensburg as well, so I'm going back to the Burg after the Oregon State comp to see him. Should be a good time. Rosemary's throwing a wedding shower for his friend that's getting married."

"A wedding, how fun."

Lyndsay's head drops, her chin nearly hitting the top of her wine glass.

"Fuck, Evan."

Lyndsay leaves after her fourth glass of wine. With neither of us working at the store, I hardly see her. She seems in good spirits. It's too bad she and Evan are fighting again. Only a matter of time before she moves back to Spokane to be with him, I suppose.

"You think she'll move to Spokane?"

"If this going back to school thing works out... maybe. She could teach while Evan does his fundraising thing. There's a Nordstrom in Spokane too."

"That's right, next to the Helly store where I got you and Lyndz the best summer jobs you ever had."

"Yes, Jon, you did hook us up working for the biggest bitch this side of Montana."

"That makes sense, but not really."

"All this Spokane talk is depressing."

"Thought you were happy to be out of school."

"Hmmph. Only when I'm sober."

"On that note, I'm outta here."

I stand up from the futon, make a move toward the kitchen, and grab my hoodie from the bar stool. Before leaving the kitchen, I take in what has to be fifty pictures on the girls' fridge going back to sophomore year. They always make me smile. There's me trying to smoke the same cigarette as Andrea on New Year's a couple of years back. That was a rough one. Angie hugging her thermos full of beer, another classic. I zip my hoodie most of the way up, and throw the hood over my head.

"All right, girly, I'll see ya later."

"OK. Don't be a stranger now."

Angie rises from her chair, walks across the living room, and wraps her arms around my waist. Her head rests against my neck. This is odd. This feels kind of good. I take my hand out of my sweatshirt pocket, place it on her cheek, and pull my head back, awaiting her rebuttal. Angie just stares into my eyes. I kiss her lightly on the lips and hold it. She doesn't pull away, and matches my pressure. We continue to lightly kiss each other without becoming anxious, or forcing the issue. Her lips are soft. I lift both her legs up, wrap them over my hips, and hold her up with my right arm as we continue to feel each other out.

"You're not complaining about the mustache now."

"Shut the fuck up."

Still cupping her, I turn left and lightly set her back against the wall, being conscious of the painting by her right side. She's light. Both her hands stroke my cheeks, and wander over my face. I sink down and begin dragging my lips across her neck. Angie begins to groan. Five years of sexual tension that has never been exercised, is finally spilling out.

Shrill voices broken up by laughter are approaching from outside, and seconds later Ashley and Liz burst through the door. My back is to them. Still holding Angie, I stop kissing her neck, and bury my face into her shoulder. The two stand silently. Ashley breaks.

"At least somebody is getting action tonight."

I've been getting more and more annoyed with J-Bird lately. Well, maybe that's just the valet job speaking, but something's on her mind and she's not talking about it, which is never the case. Later today we're meeting up with Leslie and her parents for the Chateau St. Michelle wine tour. Always a good time when they're up from California.

Delilah prances into the kitchen looking for a handout. J-Bird and I just took her to the park, so she should be exhausted. I raise my right hand in a form that usually makes Delilah sit, but for some reason she sprawls to the ground, ending up on her back with her white paws in the air. I guess if she wasn't so dumb she wouldn't be so cute. I pour a glass of water for myself, then J-Bird. She's sitting on the deck absorbing the sun. Her hair has been washed out by the summer to nearly dirty blonde. We haven't showered yet today. We never shower together at her house. I leave the kitchen for the deck, closing the door behind so Delilah doesn't get out.

"Here you go."

"Thanks."

I take a seat in the grimy deck chair next to her, chest to the sun. It's hot. I'm wincing. Pause.

"I don't like you going out with girls that I don't know."

Shit.

"Excuse me?"

"Jon, you know what I'm talking about. You left me the other day to go see a movie with this 'A-bomb.' A movie is a date, Jon. Can you see how I might be taken aback by this?"

Here we go. Use logic.

"Yes, J-Bird, I can, but the difference is I've had, and still have, good girl friends that I hang out with, she being one, whereas you don't have any guys that you're 'just' friends with. Walker is probably the closest thing."

"But Walker has a girlfriend."

"Exactly my point, he's not as accessible to you as he once was."

"And these girls are very accessible to you?"

"Because I make time for them. I make time for people in my life, mostly you. Almost all my free time goes to you, and the rest I'm left to divvy up between myself and maintaining other friendships, some of which happen to be with females. I don't think you can understand that because you have nothing to base it on. Even when Walker wasn't dating Leslie you two still never spent that much time together, unless there's something you're not telling me."

"Don't be a dick. You know everything I've done."

"Yes, and I know everything I've done, and none of qualifies as coming even close to cheating."

"Maybe not physically, but emotionally."

"What's that supposed to mean?"

"You're checking out of our relationship. Not fully involved."

"Not involved? I'm as involved as I've ever been. Every day with you is adding onto the longest relationship I've ever had. J-Bird, I will never cheat on you. You and I both know that it's impossible to not think about other people though. That isn't what's happening here. I've told you before, A-bomb is an old friend who used to live with one of my roommates a couple of summers ago. I can't believe you're not more worried about me messing around with Angie or Lyndsay. Hell, I've hooked up with Lyndsay before."

"I know them though, see them interact with you. It's different. Girls I don't know hanging out with you bother me."

I adjust in my seat, and take a gulp of water.

"I see your point, but this is how it was with Angie, and then you got to know her and it was fine. A-bomb has her own group of friends. Would you rather me tell you when I'm doing something with another girl, or not tell you? Because I haven't been telling you things because I know you get worked up, and there's nothing to get worked up about. I would never cheat on you. If I ever have strong enough feelings or desires to do something like that, I would break up with you first and I don't want to break up. You have to trust me, J-Bird, or this isn't going to work. Do you trust me?"

J-Bird takes that one in, and crosses her arms.

"Yes. Aren't you worried about me cheating on you?"

"No."

"Why?"

"Because I trust you."

"Why?"

"Because I know you love me, whatever that means, and I know what's happened to you in the past. You would never want someone to feel that way. You're a nurse, J-Bird, hurting people isn't in you."

"But don't you think other people might find me attractive?"

"Of fucking course, you've got a beautiful body and brains. I just know deep down what kind of person you are, and you would never do that."

"Well, you're right. I would never cheat on you. I just don't want to play games."

"I'm not playing games. I'm just living my life, J-Bird."

"Please stop saying 'J-Bird' after every point. That's what your dad does with your mom."

J-Bird straightens.

"Your life isn't the bachelor life anymore. You're in a fairly serious, committed relationship. There are some things that have to be sacrificed to make these things work. It's a give-and-take with both people. I know you try, and you don't realize some things because it's your first go-around with something like this, but that's how it is. If you want to be with me, you need to be with me."

She's fucking right. Goddamnit, she's smart. I need a shower.

"OK."

A-bomb is out.

I grab my other forty from Tesoro out of 723's fridge, tear the top of the brown wine bag, and wrap what's left of the small paper sack tightly around the chilled Old E's neck.

I yell, "Anybody need anything?"

Muddled negative voices come from the living room.

I walk past Moopy, still passed out on the futon, and back into the living room where Hern, Scotty, Gee, and Sherm are watching TV. Matt couldn't make it. He's with Shawnee. Scotty's switched it back to the M's game. They're all splitting leftover beer from the party last night. I sink into the couch next to Sherm.

"Hardgrove blows. Look at this shit. Does he look like he cares?"

"Easy, Gee, are we going to have a mad Gee on our hands tonight?"

"Shut the fuck up."

"Another forty, Meyer?"

"Sure, somebody has to drink 'em or else Tesoro will stop carrying them. Then what will I do? Walk an extra two blocks to Safeway, pay thirty cents more, and not get a wine bag to keep it frosty? I don't think so."

"Hardgrove sure does have nice facial hair though."

"Hey, you know what I noticed the other day walking back through DeSmet? I was looking at all those old dorm pictures from the seventies and eighties, and nearly every guy had a mustache. I couldn't fucking believe it. Seriously, like eighty percent of the guys had them. I mean, what happened?"

"Sherm, you know exactly what happened. Porn. The pornography world disgraced the mustache."

"And child molesters."

"Them too."

"Not even Kobe Bryant could bounce back from that shit."

Agreement through silence.

"We should grow mustaches."

"What are you talking about, Meyer?"

"I'm serious. If we start now we can have them fully grown by May, keep them for the first week, and then shave for graduation. C'mon, Gee, I know you're in. You're always rocking handlebars anyways."

"You know how I know you're gay, Meyer? You want to grow a mustache the final month of your collegiate career, in turn sacrificing all potential closeout ass in the process."

Pointing, "Hern, you know that wouldn't stop this face. In fact, I think it would be a pretty fun experiment to see what would happen. Fuck, if you can hook up with a chick sporting a mustache, who knows what else is possible?"

I swig. I wince. I'm getting drunk.

"I'm in, Meyer. You know I'm in."

"Nice, Gee."

"There have to be some parameters though. Trek Seattle is coming up and I'm going to be meeting with potential employers, and I don't want pubes hanging above my lip."

"Nope, only graduation or a serious job interview are allowances for shaving."

"Who says that, Gee?"

"I think I just did."

"I like it, Gee. Sorry, Hern, if you're in, you're in all the way."

"OK, I'm in. Fuckers. My future career isn't important or anything. I'm going to have a fagat on the porch."

Hern bounces up from the couch and grabs his cigs from the coffee table. Wasn't Hern going to stop smoking by graduation?

"Still trying to quit, Hern?"

The screen door slams. No answer.

"I'm in too, I guess. I hope I can get some growth before May. Two, three weeks might be pushing it."

"You'll be fine, Sherm."

"Scotty, how 'bout it?"

"I would if I could. I haven't shaved in two weeks and am still baby smooth. I'll be supporting along the way though."

"Fair enough. To Mustache May."

"To Mustache May."

Clink. Drink. Wince.

"Then it's done. Happy growing, gentlemen."

Now awake and patting his shirtless belly, Moop offers his opinion.

"You guys are fags."

FEBRUARY 29TH / 2007 / OUTSIDE BOISE

The plains of Southern Idaho extend what has to be twenty miles before morphing into foothills. A thin layer of snow covers the farmland beyond the fences alongside the highway. I haven't seen a car in forty-five minutes. I'm alone. This road goes on forever. I can't remember how long it took to get to Sun Valley in December, but I'm already an hour and half into this drive, and a growing ball of doubt is hemorrhaging in my stomach. My book-on-tape ran out on the drive to Boise, and I can't find a decent radio station. All this time for thinking will be the end of me.

Finally—hope. I've come to a four-way stop with a sign guiding me to Sun Valley. Thirty miles. No problem.

I pull into the parking lot at Formula Sports, one of my accounts, and park the Dodge Caravan. Formula is one of the more unique shops I visit because I'm pretty sure it used to be an A-frame cabin. At least that what it looks like. One can barely see into the store with all the stickers and signs in the window.

The sun is blinding, intensified by the sporadic snow piles. Locals and tourists alike are waddling around downtown. I wonder what I am. A traveling salesman, I guess.

I enter Formula to the sound of a ringing bell. Kind of obnoxious. A cute Norse-looking girl with a matching accent greets me.

"Welcome to Formula Sports. Can I help you find anything?'

"No thanks, I'm actually your Helly rep."

She smiles and clasps her hands. "Oh, I love Helly Hansen. You guys make the best stuff. Can you get me this jacket?"

She grabs one of our two women's down jacket options in white.

"Sorry, those are actually all out of stock in the warehouse."

God, she's cute.

"Is Laura in?"

"Yes, she's in the back. I'll get her."

"Thank you."

They merched their Helly nicely. All the color stories are put together in an organized fashion. I move to the back of store where Formula has the new skis for the season. After a few moments, Laura emerges from a couple of western saloon swinging doors. She's in a turquoise turtleneck and jeans; standard fair for Sun Valley.

"Hey, Jon. How are you?"

"I'm well. I'm well. Thought I had forgotten the way up here for a while."

"I know. Isn't that drive crazy? No road signs for like seventy miles. Gives you time to think though."

"That can be a good and a bad thing. I just wanted to check in and see if you had any more questions that might not have been answered at SIA?"

"Um...I don't think so. I actually have the order finished. I can give it to you now if you like?"

Hell, yes. This trip was worthwhile.

"That would be great. Could you also e-mail the order to both me and Debi for electronic purposes? I might go crazy on the way home and throw it out the window or something."

"Sure, no problem. I'll be back in a second."

"OK, great."

Laura returns with a stack of papers. She must have made doubles or something.

"I can't believe I'm about to hand over a thirty-thousand-dollar order."

What?

"Um...wow. That's great. So the line has been selling well this year?"

"It's been great. I had to choose between Helly and another company, which I won't name, and you guys came out on top."

"That makes me happy. Very happy."

This is insane.

"Um, OK. I guess I'll be on my way. Thanks so much."

"Also, Jon, Bob and I thought you did a great job presenting the line this year at SIA."

I blush. "The product is what I know, the procedure I'm still working on. Thank you though, I've had some doubts about myself and this job, and hearing things like that make it easier during the long, lonely drives."

"You're welcome and safe travels."
"Thanks. See ya next time."

  Driving back to Lyndsay's parents' house, I'm once again alone on the road, left with my thoughts. That Norwegian chick was hot. Calm down, you got a girl-friend. A great one at that. J-Bird would do anything for you. Do I deserve that? I wonder if she ever thinks about dating other guys. Sure she does. Everyone does. She's just so good at hiding it you can never tell. You're such a fucking egomaniac, Meyer.

  "Yes, Officer, I do realize I was speeding."
  His steamy breath is fogging up the Caravan's windshield. Kind of dark outside for glasses.
  "I got you at seventy-six in a sixty-five. Sound right?"
  Try seventy nine, on cruise-control.
  "Yes, sir."
  "OK, let's get your insurance and license."
  "It's a rental."
  "Whatever, just give me your license. I need to make sure you don't have any warrants out."
  "Sure. Sounds lovely."

  My last chance for gas until Boise blurs past on the right. Half tank? I'll be fine. When am I going to Portland next? I hope Lauren is working at US Outdoor. Would it be wrong to invite her out for dinner? She works at a shop I rep. All we'd talk about is the industry. I don't think that's so bad.

I hate these meetings. Why can't Debi live closer to Seattle? How can she cover all of Washington, Montana, and Northern Idaho while living on the west side of the mountains and near the Canadian border? Talk about adding some miles to a trip.

"Has Debi Little been in here?"

"Nope, haven't seen her."

"Thanks."

The Alderwood Helly store looks nice. Color stories and four-ways are presented to corporate specifications. Katherine, as much of a bitch that she is, does a nice job merching her store. I wish we could have carried some of these brands downtown. Poor souls who have to work for her. Debi enters the store while I'm in the back checking the shoes. Like me, she's wearing the current HH spring line attire.

"Hey, Jon."

She always sounds so perky even though it's obvious she's not happy to see you.

"What's up, Debi?"

"Thanks for coming north. I have to meet an account in an hour, so should we go get some coffee?"

"Sure."

We leave the store and make small talk while shaking off offers from cell phone kiosks. Out of the twenty-five food court options, only one is a coffee stand, which kind of surprises me still being close to Seattle and all.

"You want something?"

"No thanks, I don't drink coffee…at least regularly."

"OK."

Debi purchases what looks like an iced mocha while I grab a table. I unzip my pack and pull out my leather-bound organizer that houses my writing pad. The more professional I can look in front of Debi the better. The Badger (a nickname J-Bird gave her in Vegas) waddles over to the table, and hurriedly sits down. There's not much she does that isn't rushed.

"So, Jon, I'm sure you're aware of the changes going on at corporate."

"Of course."

"Well, with the cutbacks and impending merger, some things are getting changed up, um, different lines are getting drawn. They're going to redraw some of the territory lines. I don't know anything for sure just yet of what's going to happen to us, but right now the something that I do know is that my budget is getting cut. So, unfortunately, that means you have to get cut a bit. I have to slice your salary in half."

Fuck. Breathe.

"Debi, I'm not doing awful financially, but I'm not doing great. The accident last winter, my new computer, these costs have put me back indefinitely. To be honest, I'm waiting for the fall commissions to come before I'm feeling totally comfortable. And, I haven't really seen much from the sunglass commissions either."

"I know, I know. We've talked about it. They went through some turnover a couple of months ago and are just starting to get back on track."

 Pause.

"OK, so I'm getting cut back to a grand a month, and as usual my sunglass commissions are right around the corner. What else am I supposed to do?"

"I'm having to cut Shayla down too. If you want to pick up a part time job I'll allow it. At least until we know what's going on at corporate. Then I might need you back on full time again."

"Might? You don't sound too confident."

 You're going to continue fucking me, aren't you, Debi.

"You know how it is with the new owners. No one knows what they're thinking."

 I sit back in my chair to promote my displeasure. "Is that all?"

"No, you're still going to Oregon for the rail jams, right?"

"Yeah. I guess."

"If you take care of some sunglass accounts down there I'll pay you for your time on an individual account basis."

"Plus the event fee."

"Added onto the event fee. Correct."

"I've already got the tent and everything from Shayla. I'll swing by corporate on my way down and pick up some stickers. Okay. Is that it?"

"That's it."

Don't be such a dick. There really is nothing she can do...

"I'm sorry, Debi, I'm just a little flustered. Trying to internalize this. I'll e-mail you about how the rail jam went."

I close up my organizer, shove it into my pack, and leave Debi at the table. Walking back through the mall, the cell phone slingers must be able to see the anger on my face because they stay silent as I pass. It's not all Debi's fault. She's getting cut. She better be getting cut. So the winter numbers weren't quite there? How can we sell a line after this year's was so bad?

I push open the double doors and purge myself from the mall into late spring sunshine.

J-Bird, Leslie, Stos, and I stumble down the jagged steps along the south side of the house in the dark, trying to keep the noise level to a minimum as to not wake Bill and Rosemary.

"Leslie, you should've gone home with Mike. He's a good guy."

"Shut up, Jon. Just because we're all wasted, and ya'll think it's a great idea, it doesn't mean I'm hooking up with any Ellensburgers. I don't care how down home you all seem."

"J-Bird's dating one, isn't she?"

"Thanks, Stos."

"Jon's more of a transplant, Chris. He doesn't count. You Meyer boys have made it out of here. You're more worldly. That goes a long way, and makes you sooooo sexy."

"Yikes, I'll take it, sweetness, but Mike's still a good guy."

"Well you can put the topic to rest because he's not coming over here, and I'm definitely not sneaking out in the middle of night to go to his place."

"Just looking out for you."

"Well this brunette bombshell can take care of her-self and find her own man."

Snickers. Chuck the cat is the only soul to greet us from the bars. His pale orange fur has collected debris from lying on the unswept patio.

"Fair enough. I guess we'll all just go to bed, then."

We enter the house through the back door, making sure the screen door doesn't slam too loudly. Always a hassle when I was sneaking out in high school. Stos turns the outdoor light off and heads directly to the guest bedroom. Leslie turns left, into the other guest bedroom, and turns the light on. I walk up the stairs to where my bed, rather the couch, is waiting for me. J-Bird follows. Our feet lightly patter on the carpeted steps.

"Going to tell me a bedtime story?"

"Something like that."

"I really don't think sex on this couch is possible."

"Get your mind out of the gutter."

Rosemary's laid some blankets and pillows on the couch. I step out of my shoes and flop onto the flower print cushions. J-Bird sits in the gap allowed by my bent torso. I wrap my arms around her waist, and she lies back against the couch.

"So how was your first Ellensburg bar experience?"

She smiles and looks off before answering. "Just lovely. I actually did have a really good time."

"Yeah, sorry about my old classmate there. For a second I thought we were going to have some words. How dare he sit in the chair of the girl that I love."

"The girl that you love?"

"You bet."

"You love me?"

"Sure I do. I haven't felt this strongly for someone after this amount of time before."

"Four months?"

"That's big for me. I'm not a marathon dater like you."

"I hope you just remember this is the morning."

"They'll be the first words out of my mouth."

"OK, that's enough for tonight."

J-Bird grabs the fleece blanket from underneath my legs, and lays it over me. I wrap it under my body with my forearms. My eyes close.

"I love you."

"I love you too."

My mouth is absurdly dry when I wake. If the clock on the mantle is right, it's eight forty-five in the morning. My jeans and shirt are lying on the carpet next to my shoes. I must have taken them off during the night. Bill and Rosemary are mulling around in the kitchen. The girls have to be up.

I place my feet on the ground and gauge the rest my body. The hangover is holding off for now. I rise and walk through the living and dining room, into the kitchen. The day's new sun fills the house. Rosemary and J-Bird stop their conversation about nursing when I stumble in, but leave their hands cupped around their coffee mugs. Bill must have migrated to the study.

"Good morning, Jon."

"Morning Mom, J-Bird."

Everybody's smiling. The Seattle news is on the tube. I walk up beside J-Bird, lean down, and whisper, "I love you," into her ear.

"Glad you remembered."

"How could I forget?"

"Devo, it's Jon."

"Hey, Jonny. What's up?"

"I'm coming to Oregon for a rail jam. Think I can have my room tonight?"

"I don't see why not. I work until five. Meet at Beaches around five thirty?"

"Sounds good. See you there."

"Later."

"Late."

Lush green farmland, the same that you would see all the way to northern California, offers semi-satisfying scenery. I don't like how well I know this stretch of I-5.

Wondering what Breezy's up to. I send a general text seeing how she's doing. A response within two days would be a surprise. I haven't seen her the last couple of weeks, and communication has been minimal. Could it be because you might have totally freaked her out at Swan's? I wouldn't talk to you either.

Centralia blows by. They actually have some decent stores in that outlet mall. I should stop in next time.

Maybe you should also stop trying to have sex with J-Bird? What happens when you want to start something serious with someone else, and you're still sleeping with J-Bird? It would be like another breakup, except without the committed relationship, just a sex-ship. God, that might go worse than the last one. And the friendship thing is going well so far. Just chill out with her. She doesn't need to know the other stuff going on, especially Angie. It's not like you're talking to her that much either. Expectations are at an all-time low. Keep them that way. If something happens, it happens, and it will probably be a great time, but definitely a bad idea. No sex has fewer ramifications than one night of pleasure. Then it's settled. No sex with J-Bird.

My phone, that has been resting under my right leg, begins to vibrate. No light so it's a text. I grab the phone keeping one hand on the wheel to continue negotiating the packed interstate, and raise it to my face.

It's A-bomb.

"*Want to play some tennis?*"

"*I'm on my way to Oregon. Won't be back until Monday.*"

"*Travel safe.*"

"*Will do.*"

I exit I-5 just before crossing the bridge into Oregon, and head East to Devo's little condo community. I veer right and cruise along the community's border until pulling into Beaches' parking lot. As usual, there's quite the crowd for happy hour. I hope Devo's landed a table.

Inside it's loud, talking heads at every table. Flower shirts on the servers, *Burgers in Paradise* on the stereo, bamboo jutting out from everywhere—I understand. No sign of Devo or an open seat. A floral-clad waitress, young, braces, and all smiles, approaches me.

"Hi, welcome to Beaches. Can I help you with something?"

"Yes, I'm looking for, well… a dorky-looking guy my age…in a suit."

She walks toward the bar but stops before entering.

"The next room. He's got a seat. Lucky you."

"He always was the responsible one. Thanks."

I turn the corner and see Devo, eyes upward watching a baseball game. He's still in his work garb as I had guessed. Always a nice foil in his Men's Warehouse suit, tie, and buffed dress shoes.

"How's my banker doing?"

"Your banker is tired. How was the drive?"

"The usual. Spent my time filling loneliness with anger for truckers. I can't do that drive anymore, man. It's killing me."

"Well, you're here now. Drink up."

Devo pushes a Heifeweizen my direction that I hadn't noticed upon sitting down. That's kind of him to order for me. Well, I am going to be paying for it anyways. I take the lemon wedge from the rim of the pint glass, squeeze, and drop it into the murky, golden beer.

"Thanks. Anything new in the community banking world?"

"Can't say there is. Just checked up on some accounts today. Pretty boring stuff. I wouldn't have minded being in a car for half the day."

"I don't know if your accounts would've wanted me to show up at their door though."

"That's true."

Braces comes back to the table.

"You gentlemen ready to order?"

"Ah yeah, I think so. I'll do the spicy chicken mac and cheese, and the calamari. Devon?"

"Geesh. I think I'll do the same."

"OK, that will be right out."

Devo looks after her.

"Get those braces off and we might be talking."

"So how is Steffi?"

"She's fine. The exciting life of a Portland State R.A. is still wearing on her, but she's almost done. Then, I don't know."

"Don't think you'll stick together after she graduates?"

"I'm pretty sure she wants to move in, and that's not going to happen."

"I see, you only like house guests once a month who aren't gunning for a wedding ring."

"Exactly."

"Sounds heartbreaking."

Devo downs a couple of gulps of his own Hef.

"It will be for someone."

I pay the bill, essentially my rent for the night, and we hop into my car and make the short two-block drive to Devo's condo. The bank he works at is just down the street, so he walks to work every day. That also means he doesn't make it out of this community all that much.

"Want to tub?"

"Sure."

I haul my bag from the Element after parking, and we head into Devo's three-story, half-committed bachelor pad. Once inside, as custom, I take off my shoes and quickly take the first set of stairs. Devon's painted another wall dark beige in the living room since the last time I've been here. It looks good.

"Have you met Terry yet?"

"Excuse me?"

Devo references a vase sitting atop a designer book shelf. Inside the vase swims a merlot-colored fish, at home with its stick of bamboo.

"It's a Japanese fish. I don't know if it's a boy or a girl, so I went with a transsexual name. Terry is also short for Teriyaki."

"Well done, Devo."

"It's nice to have someone to come home to."

"I'm sure it is. I'm going to go change into my suit."

"All right, see you back here in a few."

Devo and I cross the street outside his condo to the community fitness center, which contains the hot tub. Devo's wearing the red Helly Hansen top I gave him on one of my winter trips for use of the guest bedroom. Can't buy dinner every time I'm down here. Good to see he's putting it to use. He hops into the tub while I crank the bubbles for the fifteen minutes. I test the steaming water with my right foot before slinking all the way in. Never been much of a hot water guy, at least to the level of others. J-Bird always preferred the shower substantially hotter than me; in turn, she would often get most of her bathing done by the time I joined her in hopes of avoiding the death freeze that comes with my aversion to scolding hot water.

"So what else is going on, Meyer? Still think you made the right decision opting for the single life?"

"It seems so. I've got the right kind of problems. I'm trying to manage a couple of different girls, and I just don't know if I'm up for it. If I had a real job that actually took up some time then I'd really be fucked."

"Still talking to J-Bird?"

"More like is she still talking to me...yeah. I'm just so horny, I called her one lazy afternoon to see if she wanted to come over and, *make love all afternoon*."

"No shit!"

"Oh yeah, she declined. In fact, she started laughing...I don't blame her. It was actually refreshing to hear her laugh instead of the grief I usually cause her. She politely said, *no* and left for her shift at the hospital. The positive that did come out of later texting though was that she's not totally opposed to sleeping with me, it just has to happen '*naturally*.'"

"Naturally? What's that mean?"

"The sex to seem random, not planned—not like I'm calling her over like a prostitute."

"She doesn't want to feel like she's being used."

"Right, how dare she?"

"I know, listening to her instincts. What's up with that?"

"So what else is out there?"

"This little cute thing, nineteen-year-old SPU student."

"How'd you meet her?"

"At Evo, where I used to work. I thought she was our age. She's really hot, and she's really cool, but she's only nineteen! I just can't get past that. Cute blonde little thing. Breezy. The problem with her is that she's so hard to get a hold of. She's not on Facebook or MySpace, so that takes away two avenues of flirtation, leaving me just the phone. I've been balancing random calls with timely texts. Nothing much has come of it. She doesn't usually get back to me for two or three days. I think I should just give up on that one. I don't know if I could date a girl with a couple of years of college left again either. The stress of school on J-Bird, even though she handled it well, was at times fairly unnerving for both of us."

Devon's now floating, resting his head on the edge of the hot tub.

"And...who else?"

"Who have you been talking to? OK...and this girl A-bomb who I met a couple of years ago at Holdz-worth's place. She's just super nice and pretty chill. Not the hottest thing out there, but cute. Olive skin, petit little body. Pretty fun in bed too 'cause she's one of those chicks that goes through a complete transformation once she starts getting turned on. I've never heard panting like that before. Also, when we're hooking up and I look at her closed eyes, you can tell she's just off in some other world. If it's not with me, that's fine. She also keeps a bedside table stash of condoms. What do you think of that?"

"I think it means she likes safe sex."

"But how much of it do you think she's having?"

"You mean is she sleeping with other guys too?"

"Well to have a stash of condoms alongside your bed means you're having a fair amount of sex...right? And we've only done it twice over a period of probably a month."

"Intriguing."

"It's really none of my business, and I have no right to talk with the way I'm currently living my life. I thought you might have an opinion on it."

"My opinion is she likes the cock, and sometimes it might not be yours."

"I see."

"And Angie? How's Angie?"

I raise my freshly pruned hands out of the tub, and pull them down my face, hoping for a relaxed feeling to come over me.

"It happened. We finally kissed...well kissed more than the New Year's debacle a couple of years ago. This was full-on passionate, making out. That is until Ashley and Liz came in."

"What do you mean?"

"Angie and I were in the living room...having some fun...when Ashley and Liz came through the front door."

"Well what'd you do after that?"

"I got flustered, said my good-byes, and left."

"Just like that?"

"Just like that."

"Have you seen her since?"

I attempt to mimic Devo's relaxed position, but end up taking in a mouthful of chlorine as my head slips off the edge. Devo doesn't notice, and must be thinking that I'm taking my time to answer that one. Once I clear my mouth of tub water, I finally get to his question.

"Yeah, we've hung out a couple of times during the day. Nothing at night. It's not awkward or anything yet, which is nice. She leaves for Peru soon so I think things are going to work themselves out."

"You mean she'll leave and you won't have to worry about it anymore?"

"That's a little harsh, but yeah. I still got to tell Munroe. He needs to know. He's put as much into that as I have."

"You're a piece of work, Jonny."

"Yup. I just wish I knew how I work."

The bubbles time out and fizzle away. The sun is setting. The fluorescent hot tub lights illuminate our wavy, pale legs.

"Shall we?"

"Sure."

We rise out of the tub, board shorts sticking to our legs. I grab one of Devon's thick, beige towels and wrap it around my waist. Nice towels. A puddle forms underneath me. The cool evening air bites as we tiptoe back to the condo.

The night has turned cool, but my face is warm. Matt and I are sitting on the girls' stoop trying to finish our second forty. It's not going down easy. The cops have left. The party is just getting going back inside Angie and Shawnee's, at least the music has been turned up. The smokers are over by the fence in a circle, a haze resting over them. A couple of sophomore lacrosse guys are pissing on the neighbor's house.

"Think you'll marry Shawnee?"

"I hate you. No."

"Than why are you together?"

"We're…I'm comfortable. We've talked about it, trying to keep it going after college, but I think we both know it's not going to last. We work when we're together, but it's tough when there's separation."

Swig. Wince. I pull the forty out of its bag. Halfway done. I exhale. Straggling partygoers parade through the alley, laughing loudly and falling over themselves.

"Well that's interesting. So you're just going to keep riding it out until Oregon?"

"Yup. She's going to come to Coos Bay and help us move in, then it's down to California for her."

"That's nice of her. A lady's touch will not go unappreciated."

Hern puts his cigarette out and walks up the stairs. Matt and I shift, letting him pass in between. The music, Sinatra, sneaks out when Hern opens the door.

"What about you...if you could marry a GU chick, who would it be?"

Swig. Wince.

"I've talked to Hern about this before. I asked him the same question I did you, but about Jacki. Of the girls here, that I've had experience with, I'd have to give the advantage to Liv, and then maybe Angie."

"So Angie's up there?"

"Yeah, you know we get along fine, understand each other, I think. She's got her own thing going on, which is nice. I hate chicks that just leach energy off you because they got nothing going on themselves."

"Weren't you working on Liv pretty tough first semester?"

"Absolutely. Talked to her a couple of times over the summer about how we'd fallen off since freshman year. Thought I could get that magic back, but soon realized freshman year was a long time ago. Fuck... Liv's so great. Too great. Too good for me, like, literally too nice of a person for me."

"She's one hell of a lady."

"Anyways, every time I would try to get some face time with her this fall, fucking Tom would show up. He's in love with her and I was too horny to put up a good fight and wait around. He won. My mom still hasn't forgiven me for fucking that one up. Asks about her all the time. Midwestern girl. She loved her."

Swig.

"So that's it. Liv and Angie, in that order."

"That's not a bad list."

"I wonder what percentage of college couples who graduate dating actually get married?"

"I don't know...maybe ten?"

"Sounds about right. I mean, I just look at my uncle who got married at forty-five, and she's absolutely the right woman. It took him twenty something years after college to find the right person. I really do think you know when you've found the right one, right away."

"Some switch clicks. Ha-ha, that rhymes."

Swig. Purse lips.

"Something like that. So far, every girl I've dated I've known it wasn't going to last from the start. I just waited it out until some problem arose, ended it, and chalked it up as another learning experience. I'm just waiting for the girl who's going to make me miserable again because I can't live without her."

"Wait, you've been miserable over a girl before? Jon Meyer?"

"Danae Robertson. Seventh grade. We dated for about a month, you know, held hands and shit, and then she sent the assassin Sydney Drinkwater to break up with me after school." I turn to Matt. "When Sydney came around, you knew it was bad news. She did a lot of girls' bidding. Danae's still the only girl that I've dated that I've started to like more as the relationship went on, instead of vice versa. Even in seventh grade, getting dumped hurt bad. I knew after that, I never wanted to get dumped again. I was always going to be the one doing the dumping. The one in control."

"Do you still talk to her?"

"Hell no. I think she's still in the Burg. And what would I say? 'Hey, Danae, yeah, Jon Meyer here. *Just wanted to let you know that because you broke up with me I've never been able to completely commit myself to another girl for fear of rejection. Thanks.*' That actually does have a nice ring to it."

"I think that might make Danae Robertson's night. You should do it, kind of like the twelve steps thing where you have to come clean with everyone you've ever wronged, except she's the one who wronged you. That analogy doesn't work, but still, I think Danae needs to hear from you."

"In time. In time. Maybe at the ten year?"

Angie pops her head out the door.

"Hey boys, ready to head to the bars?"

"Can we take our forties?"

Swig.

"I don't want to be seen with you drinking that thing, Jon."

"You disgust me."

"Right back at ya."

Another standard night at the Bulldog, followed by another standard night at Jack and Dan's: smiling faces, a pitcher of beer drowned, and observations on who's taking who home.

Matt and Shawnee break for his place while Angie and I climb the stairs next door to hers, slinking into the duplex. Red cups and empty beer bottles cover every tabletop and windowsill. *Summer Wind* is still on the stereo. There's my couch. It's the only couch I've ever slept on that my six-two frame fits on. I flop on the blue and gold patterned cushions, and fully extend my legs for a stretch. Angie heads into the kitchen. She got dressed up tonight.—a little tank and jeans. Looks good. Too bad she's still hung up on her ex.

"Water?"

"Please."

My feet are dangling off the couch, and I lose my sandals in preparation for sleep. No spins. That's nice. I'm actually not too drunk. A blanket is resting above me. I grab it and do a full roll to get completely wrapped. Angie returns with my water, and it actually takes quite the effort to get my arms out from the blanket.

"Thanks."

"You're welcome."

I roll onto my side and Angie fills the new empty space.

"Nice work on the blanket."

"I've been here before. I know the program."

"Yes, you have, and yes, you do. Not coming up tonight?"

"I think I'm good down here. Don't want you to suffer through my snoring."

Angie dips down and lightly pecks my lips, pulls away, and lingers, waiting for my answer. She's got to be drunk. I don't kiss back. My breath is awful.

"MMM...nope. Not like this, Angie. We've been drinking. Not like this."

She hovers, considers my answer, and leaves me for the stairs and her room.

"Good night, Jon."

I muster, "Night, darling," and pass out.

MAY 17ᵀᴴ / 2007 / CORVALLIS

Oregon State's campus is on fire. Students are mulling around happy to be outside and enjoying a nice day. Girls are wearing just enough to not get arrested. Is there anything better than a spring day on a college campus? It's another one of those seventy-five degree days that feels like ninety. The black tee I'm wearing doesn't help. Is it unprofessional to not wear a shirt while working the booth? It is a rail jam.

I illegally park next to the Cricket van, another sponsor, and begin unloading. My booth spot is a couple of hundred yards from the car, and on my first load I'm already sweating. Ryan, the organizer, wants the sponsors set up by one. I'm a little early, so that shouldn't be a problem. Two dump trucks full of snow are parked in the epicenter of the quad. A contingent of riders has started shoveling the snow onto the massive scaffolding. OSU's Roman-styled student union building, and all twenty-something columns, serve as the backdrop of the event. Students come and go from every direction. If they're not talking on their cell phones, they're texting. I've never seen anything like this before, even at Gonzaga. I give a couple of students some beanies to help me raise the tent, and I'm in business. Stickers, posters, conversation…all can be found here, at the big red Helly Hansen tent.

I'm out all my stickers before the event even starts, and the posters will be gone soon. The quicker they're gone, the less attention I have to give to people walking by, and I can just sit back and watch the event.

The riders looked shaky in warm-up, but I doubt any of them have been riding on snow this sticky lately. No way would I do anything like this. The course starts out with two rail options, allowing for multiple lines to be formed, and then has a flat rail option at the bottom for those with enough speed. Not too many were carrying enough speed at the bottom for the final rail in warm-ups. Ryan found your standard obnoxious MC to call the event. The guy's at the top of the scaffolding intermixed with the riders, dropping people's nicknames like we're supposed to know who they are. Today's hottest hip-hop music blares from two large speakers. I never have understood this: Two sports that are completely dominated by white folks, skiing and snowboarding, somehow have adopted hip-hop as its music style of choice. I'm not saying they should be blaring Boyz II Men or anything, but some Zeppelin would be nice every once in a while.

Co-eds continue to cross through the quad, everyone debating whether to stay and watch the madness that is going on, or continue to class. Once in a while, a couple of people that know each other will run into one another, and strike up a conversation. I'm guessing about what's happening tonight or what pages need to be read for ethics. That's it. That is now what I miss most about college. The random run-ins. Not the parties. Not hooking up with a wide variety of girls. I miss walking through campus, thinking about nothing in particular, and then running into someone you haven't seen for a while, and then just kicking it on a bench, talking about the party that night, or where the other roommates are. That's college. *What do you really have to do*? Where in your life will you have so many people you know, congregated in one geographical area ever again? Never.

But you don't realize that then, or at least until senior year.

They're all smiling, laughing. Each one of them not knowing what life outside the collegiate experience holds for them. Am I jealous? A little. Do I want to tell every one of them that life gets mildly worse after you shake hands with the dean? No. That's something that is unique to each person. How you handle that first fall without parties lining up one weekend after another. People you used to have class with every day are now starting careers on the other side of the country.

By six my posters are gone and the competition is winding down. If I leave now I can make it to Ellensburg by twelve. Thanks for the memories, OSU.

I've already driven past the site of my accident three months ago when I hit Sedas Pass. Dry roads make for calmer nerves. Pine trees line the two-lane highway on both sides, abruptly ending the light glow of my high beams. The tent and its frame in the back are sliding with every windy turn. Only a few trucks have passed going south. A slow night for Sedas.

A brown blur enters my field of vision to my right and quickly hovers in front of the Element. The voice in my head says, *"Keep going straight—do not veer,"* and whatever it was, has now impacted the front of the SUV. I'm alive. I'm still driving straight. That's good. Adrenaline pushes through my body, sharpening my vision on the now darkened highway. Slow down. Calm down. Slow down. Let's make it to Ellensburg alive. Rosemary needs you for the wedding shower tomorrow.

What I'm guessing was a hawk of some sort has lost the battle with the Element. In a losing effort however, it has taken life from my right front headlight. Fuck.

Once I stop shaking, I pull my phone from under my leg to call Angie and tell her what happened. She'll get a laugh out of this. No reception. Damnit. Glad that wasn't worse. This car is cursed. I'm selling it the first chance I get. Weak light illuminates a mileage sign. Eighty miles to Ellensburg.

I arrive at the lifeless house around twelve. The porch light is my welcoming committee. I don't even bother to unload my luggage bag, and head straight for the door. Nine hours in the car today. Not bad. Not a record, but not bad.

Quietly, I open and shut the back door, and turn off the porch light. There's a note on the white board from Chris saying he's going downtown. He must not be back yet, so I turn the porch light back on.

The hallway is dark but I know where I'm going. I stick my right hand out to touch the wall and walk forward, waiting for the elbow of the hallway that will take me right, and lead me to my old room. Showering can wait. I enter the bedroom and smell the smell that will never leave me; not quite the same dinge of Grandpa's old house, but eerily similar. I think it's the curtains. I step out of my shorts and sandals, lift my shirt off, and collapse into my brother's old twin bed, and succumb to sleep.

The Meganhardts are on vacation, and J-Bird has been charged with house-sitting instead of her usual duties of monitoring the Meganhardts' children. They have a pleasant little bungalow located in North Ballard that's kind of a hassle to get to from Wallingford, but we're having fun playing house while they're gone. Their two older black labs, Jet Texas and Abigail, are also watching the house with us.

"What do you want to do for dinner tonight?"

"I was thinking having Leslie and Swan over for some BBQ. What do you think?"

"That sounds good. I'll call Leslie."

"K. I'll get Swan on the horn."

I move from the kitchen to the orange-and-red-walled living room, giving J-Bird some privacy on her call. The hardwood floors are smooth under my bare feet.

"Swanson, what you up to?"

"Nothing, over in the U District."

"Want to BBQ?"

"Sure, where at?"

"Over in Ballard."

"Cool. Be there in thirty. Hey, is Leslie going to be there?"

"Think so, J-Bird's talking to her now."

I look back around the corner and J-Bird nods.

"Cool. Just meet Leslie at their place. She'll drive."

"Okeydokey. Late."

I creak back into the kitchen where J-Bird's sitting at the table on the phone. She and Leslie are having a lively conversation. I mouth to J-Bird that I'm heading to the store, and she waves me off.

I return with enough meat and beer to feed the party. I'm a provider. Only the finest food and beverage on a valet/sales associate's salary. J-Bird's feeding the dogs.

"What'd you get, babe?"

"Some steaks with special seasoning, a couple of chicken breasts, and some beer."

"Beer?"

"Yeah, shit...sorry. Well, you drink it sometimes. This whole allergic to wheat thing really works against my love of carbs."

J-Bird stands and moves to the fridge.

"I think the Meganhardts have some wine. It's fine."

"Sorry. Again. I'm going to light up the Q."

Swan pops through the front door. He's in cargo shorts, some random print tee, and leather sandals. Lately, he's been keeping a beard at half growth. People often mistake us for brothers, which I take as a compliment. He's a good-looking guy. Leslie follows behind. They're laughing about something Leslie said.

"Swanson, get out here and help me with the grill."

"You know it."

"Good to see you too, Jon."

Smiling, "Right. Hi Les. Swan, Grab a couple of beers too, will ya?"

"Affirmative," he answers, dragging out the "a."

I slide open the porch door, step onto the wood deck that could use some staining, and place the plate of meat on the grill's prep table. Swan follows with four beers, and closes the door. Dusk settles in and the temperature outside is perfect. I turn the propane on and light the grill.

"What's J-Bird worked up about?"

"She's allergic, well, kind of allergic to wheat. She can eat pasta and drink beer without dying, but it makes her sick. I don't know why, but I can never remember when I'm buying food for us. I guess it's because she still consumes it most of the time. I can't make many meals that don't include pasta. It's kind of my thing."

"Huh, that's weird. So she'll voluntarily take it in, knowing that later she'll feel bad?"

"Yup."

"What a champ."

"I know."

Through the glare of the patio's sliding glass door, Leslie and J-Bird are sitting at the table enjoying some red wine. Leslie's latest fashion is the spring dress. This one looks to be a blueberry tone with a white flower print. Interesting.

"So what do you think of Leslie? Pretty cool chick, right?"

"Yeah, super cool."

"This double-date thing has really been working out so far. Let me tell you, I've been enjoying it. Please don't fuck it up, Swan."

"I'll try not to, but if she's start getting too close to these insides," Swan wags a finger, "uh uh. It's over."

"I understand, still not ready for a full go after ending it with Jevin?"

"Just looking to have fun, man. Wasn't it you eight months ago telling me I needed to be single so we could run the town?"

"Maybe."

"And look at you now, playing house with J-Bird...in someone else's house. How's it feel?"

"Well, we got a nice piece of property here, two dogs, two kids. Can't say life is bad, Swan."

"Seriously though, according to your previous theory if you're with J-Bird, that means you think this is a chick you can marry. Is this true?"

"Um, yeah. It's not like I can say I've never thought about it. J-Bird's great. She makes me laugh. We're good in bed. She's going to have an economically stable career once she graduates, and I know she's good with kids. I'm just so far away from being at a point where I think I could ask someone to marry me."

"Economically stable?"

"Yeah, that's my dad talking. Don't even get me started. I have a list from him of thirteen things every successful spouse should bring to the table, other than steaks."

"Scary."

"Maybe, I mean my parents are great together, whatever sick formula they've drawn up."

I throw all forms of meat on the grill, and savor in the sizzling noise coming from the grill's searing heat.

"How long you going to leave those steaks on?"

"Eight and six. The one other thing my dad taught me. Eight minutes one side, six the other. Usually produces a nice medium-rare."

"Sounds like your dad has things figured out."

"Unfortunately so, because growing up I got to hear just how figured out he has it." I lower my voice for effect, "'*Chris, Jon, turn the TV down. I want to tell you boys something.*'"

"Yikes."

"It's not so bad, only took me twenty years before I realized he does shit like that out of love rather than sheer annoyance of his sons."

I do one last check to make sure the meats are properly spaced.

"C'mon, let's see what the girls are up to."

Swan yanks on the sliding door and I follow him back into the pale yellow kitchen.

"How was work today, Miss Leslie?"

"Just fine, Jon. I think we had a total of five people come into the store, and two of them returned things. Clothes *you* probably sold to them."

"Very nice, I'm sure you wowed them with your customer service skills."

"Only the best from the assistant manager. I don't think I stood up the whole day. I was firmly planted on the back table."

Swan looks at me for my bottle opener, which I use to open his second beer, and then mine. Don't let this get awkward. I need this to work. Man friends dating good girlfriends—I've never had that before. It's perfection. They seem to be doing well. Don't fuck this up, Swan.

"So, Leslie, it's me and you in the store tomorrow. Tell me, what are we not going to do?"

J-Bird settles into her wine a little more.

"Well, Jon. First, you can plan on not stocking the floor. Second, feel free to linger and lean at any point during the day. And third, ten Helly Bucks for hitting your sales goal."

"I can't wait."

J-Bird and I are lying in the Meganhardts' bed when the squeaking commences in the attic. It is an old bed, but they're really going at it. I smile and look for J-Bird's reaction, but she's lying still, seemingly oblivious to the boisterous sex our two friends are having.

"Everything OK? Don't you hear what's going on?"

"I hear what's going on, I just have other things on my mind."

"Like what?"

"Like why you enjoy talking to Leslie more than me. You should have seen you two at dinner tonight. In your own little world. Justin and I both looked at each other in amazement. What is it between you two?"

Seriously?

"Seriously."

"We're just friends, J-Bird, that I guess have a little livelier conversation when we're around each other. We've talked about this before. Leslie's a little over-bearing sometimes, but you also shy away. I'm sorry if we got a little carried away tonight, but you need to be more assertive. Leslie's a strong personality and needs the attention. You know this more than I do."

"Sometimes, when other people are around I wish you would just please me for once. Let others have their own conversation."

"I like entertaining, I like people to feel involved."

"Then get me involved. Get me involved the next time because right now it feels like we're not even in the same room sometimes."

Not even in the same room? That's a little dramatic. Be careful. This could get bad. What does she want to hear?

"Um."

No. Give yourself some time. Let's think. How is she feeling right now? Alone. Unwanted. Make her feel better about herself.

"You know I met Leslie first, and then you, and who did I choose? I'm with you, J-Bird, but Leslie and I still work together and experience a lot of the same stuff on a day-to-day basis, so we're constantly going to have work things to talk about. I'm sorry about tonight. I was just so happy Swan came over."

In rhythm, the thumping from above continues.

"Well, you're my boyfriend, and I want it to feel like you're my boyfriend when we're around each other."

"OK, but I need you to be more honest during these types of things. As much as I like to think that I understand a woman's psyche, I still need help. If we're out somewhere or throwing a party, and you want my attention, tell me you want my attention. Don't stare at me from the corner of the room waiting for me to look at you while I continue in a conversation, and get pissy about it later."

Uh oh. That came out a little harsh. J-Bird rolls over, pulling sheets with her, and begins to sob. Fuck me. Quickly, I wrap her in my arms and pull her in. Swan's picking up his pace upstairs. Get her, buddy.

"I'm sorry. That came out wrong. I just need you to be more vocal out there, instead of in here. You know I don't like talking about these things before bed. This type of thing has happened a couple of times now, and I just can't fix it unless you tell me when it's happening. Otherwise, I'm just going to keep talking with whoever I'm talking with. Does that make sense?"

The sobbing is starting to slow. Yes.

"I guess so."

J-Bird firmly grabs my elbow and pulls. I feel like I'm going to suffocate her at this rate. The squeaking from above slows, and eventually stops. I glance at the clock. Seven minutes for Swan. J-Bird's sniffles fade as well, allowing her to muster, "I love you."

"I love you too."

My eyes open and move directly to the clock. Nine. I can deal with that. I hop out of bed, tie on my light blue terry cloth bathroom robe that stays at the house, and climb the stairs to the kitchen where Chris is already on his laptop, eating a bowl of Chex. The morning Sportscenter is muted on the island TV.

"What's up, Stos? How was Portland?"

"Good time, caught up with Eric and some of the old UP guys. You remember Eric, right?"

"Oh yeah, Jen Hab's ex-boyfriend?"

"Yup. How'd the comp go yesterday?"

I dig into the cupboard and grab out some Honey Bunches of Oats. Way to go, Mom. You knew I was coming home.

"So so. It was so hot. Just handed out SWAG and took off. Working those things by yourself is never that much fun. Having to look at unattainable college chicks all day doesn't help either."

"Ah, the first days of spring on a college campus... how I miss them."

"You've been out of school longer than me and are still yearning? Shit."

"Why do you think I'm going to grad school?"

I turn from my bowl of cereal. "To better the world?"

"Well, that too."

"Talking to the tree guys in Panama?"

"Yeah, we're about to Skype."

"All right, I'll eat my cereal in silence. Are you mowing the lawn today?"

"You're doing the back and I got the front."

"Fair enough. Mom outside?"

"Yeah. Hey, what the fuck did you hit with your car?"

"I don't want to deal with that now. Let me eat my cereal in peace."

I bound back down the stairs after my two bowls of cereal, leaving Chris to his conference call, and burst out the screen door into a sunny Ellensburg morning. Rosemary's in the garden planting some veggies.

"Morning, Mother."

"Oh, Jon. You're up. I figured you got in late and I didn't want to wake you."

"Thanks for that, even though Chris' old bed didn't do much to comfort me. His body shape is molded into that mattress. The hip alignment isn't even close."

"He did steal the bigger bed."

"The kid comes home once a year and thinks he can take my guest bed."

"First come, first serve. No favorites in this house."

"Come on, Mom, I'm the one still spending the majority of my time in the United States. That has to count for something."

"Me buying groceries isn't payment enough?"

Rosemary turns back to her garden and places a baby plant of some kind in a vacant hole.

"Good call. So what time are people coming over for the wedding shower?"

"You need to be dressed and ready by five. Are you doing anything today other than the chores I have listed?"

"Chris and I were planning on hiking The Ridge."

"Well be back by four."

"You got it."

Chris continues a blistering pace that I'm having problems keeping up with. I thought I was in shape. We're almost to the trees that will offer some shade from the spring sun. The Kittitas Valley lays itself out below, showing off its shades of green, boxed into fields of hay. Mt. Stuart peaks with snow to the North.

"So what's up with you, little bro? How's Angie?"

"She's good. We've started messing around, well, at least once. Sorry, she's off the market for ya. I always thought that if you went to graduate school at UW you two should date. Looks like she might be settling for the younger Meyer."

"And J-Bird?"

"Oof, we're talking, so that's good, I guess. Trying to keep options open. I'm starting to think that if we start messing around, or even continue talking, that I'm never going to really let her go though. She's going to have to start dating someone before I'll stop thinking we'll eventually hook up. That's not healthy, is it?"

"I don't think so. Here comes some older brother advice. Chill the fuck out. Leave the girls alone, get your shit together, and make some money."

"That's a little different than Bill would put it, but I think I understand you."

"It's different because it's not in a letter."

"Correct. So how's your Panamanian firecracker?"

"She wants commitment. She wants me to come visit her every month. Demands, demands, demands. But she's on fire, Jon. Latino women are wild, and moody, and I can't get enough."

"I'm sorry. Sounds like a vicious cycle."

Chris stops and turns to me.

"I can't break up with her. It's impossible. She won't let it happen, and I don't have the balls to say 'no more.' I'm a ball-less man when I'm in Panama."

Chris turns back up the hill, and starts chugging again. The dirt trail is sprinkled with wild flowers to each side.

"Maybe this whole tree-planting thing needs to be moved to another country?"

"That's the best business idea I've heard in a while."

Meeting a brisk wind, we finally reach the top. The temp is cool enough to warrant a shirt. Chris and I return our tees over our shoulders. I walk behind a bush to piss, leaving my brother to the view. His hands are still on his hips when I return.

"Sign the book?"

"Not yet."

I grab the rusted green tin that houses The Ridge's logbook for summits. The journal is already open to the last page.

"Rusty and Krissy made it up already today... in the morning."

Chris gives no answer. He's taking in the view. There are multiple pens lying in the bottom of the tin. I snag the sparkly pink one for no reason, sit down on one of the large rocks scattered around the top, and inscribe "*ANOTHER MEYER MEN SUMMIT—C + J.*"

"When did you start writing in all caps? You know Dad does that?"

"Junior year I realized I couldn't read my own notes from class, so I started writing in caps."

"So that's why you failed English?"

"Exactly.

We look over the valley that raised us for eighteen years of our lives.

"It's nice, right?"

"My friends in DC don't understand what space looks like. Towns just run together all the way up the East Coast. They have no concept of *space*."

"I don't think I'll ever move from the Northwest."

"I want to end up here too, just need to take care of some things first."

"Like becoming president?"

"Yup."

"When that happens, you should know I'm not coming with you, to DC that is."

"Why not?"

"Because people over there think the only Washington is the one they're living in. It's obnoxious."

"It's not as bad as you think…maybe it is? It's just different priorities. They're more concerned with where you come from, more like who you come from, and how much money you have. Out here everyone is just more laid back. Not right, not wrong, just different."

"I don't know how you do it…watch sports so late at night?"

"Me neither…me neither." Chris swivels. "Let's get home before Mom has our ass."

Familiar faces start showing up. The Shaws come in droves. Casey and Anne first, followed by the brother's and parents. Casey's cleaned up his goatee and cut his hair. That's nice. Grandma Max, the head of the family, even made the party. The Mattocks are fashionably late as usual, but offer comedic relief once present. Karyn is already going for the red wine. Gotta get those tannins. Teet, Goob, and Dave all come in the same car. Dave's put some weight back on. That's no good.

"Jon, you're home! Come here! You give the best hugs."

Phyllis Shaw, the mother of the groom and longtime Momma Mafia Czar, is quickly approaching. I give her my patented friend-of-the-family hug, hopefully not disappointing.

"Hey, Phyllis. You have to be happy. Another son tying the knot."

"Half the fun are these little get-togethers so all you boys can see each other. I miss having all of you sitting in my kitchen, keeping me up on all the gossip."

The smile never leaves.

"So that's why you would invite us over without Rusty knowing?"

"Sometimes I just had to know what you boys were up to."

"Or who had the hots for Rusty? I guess the last time we did something like this it was for him and Krissy."

"That's right. Now when is your mother going to be able to throw a wedding shower for you?"

I spot Shawzie out on the porch.

"Uh, haha...not for a while at this point. I'm going to go talk to that son of yours. See you when the games start."

"OK, Jon. Rusty's been looking forward to you being home."

"It's good to be home."

I leave Phyllis and walk through the screen door onto the porch. More and more people are arriving, making the alley look like a used car lot. Some of Anne's friends hop out of the standard Ellensburg vehicle, a jacked-up truck that eats money. Rosemary wanted to have Anne feel as comfortable as possible amongst a tight-knit Ellensburg crowd that grew up together, so the invitation of her friends along with booze are supposed to help. Rusty sees me coming from the kitchen to the porch, and nods when I offer another beer. I need to be buzzed to get through this.

I steal Mirror Ponds from the cooler along with a bottle opener. Goob, Dave, and Teet have migrated to Shawzie since I leaned down for the beers. That was fast. Chuck the cat is sprawled in the middle of the yard.

"Gentlemen."

"Meyer, good to see you know your way back over the mountains. Nice stache too."

I hand Shaw his beer, and uncap mine.

"C'mon, Dave, hasn't been that long since I've been in the Burg."

"Maybe it's just been a while since I've seen you."

"That's probably it."

"What are you boys up to? Teet, done with school yet?"

"One more quarter."

"Then back to Dusty's?"

"No way, I'm done with that shit. I see you're still drinking the dark stuff."

"Teet, just cause it's not Bud Light and actually tastes good, doesn't mean it's shit. We've already been over this."

"You won't see me drinking that shit."

"More for me."

"Shawzie, wasn't too long ago you and Krissy were being forced onto that living room couch?"

"It wasn't that bad, Glas. Casey will be fine."

"I don't know, all the Mafia members are here. The women who know everything about everyone. There are some stories that can come out."

"Not about us, though, so I don't care."

"Not like you did anything that bad, Goob. Not like any of us did anything bad. We were the good ones, remember? Compared to our brothers...angels."

Rosemary is now motioning from the living room for the party to move inside. It's time for gifts and whatever games she's come up with. Standing beside her, Bill's icy feelings toward the shower have melted away with a couple of beers, and as much as he denies enjoying a nugget of gossip, these little get-togethers help keep him in the know.

"All right, fellas, here we go."

I corral the crowd into the living room, leaving the shade of the porch for the air-conditioned house.

Around twenty-five people are in a circle around the living room, with Anne and Casey on the love seat in front of the fireplace. Anne's opened up another present with a "horse" theme, I think this one is a soap dish, and I can't help but think about the parallels of when I was growing up and all anybody wanted to talk to me about was golf. Casey just looks uncomfortable, and obviously wants the shower to be over. The only present that's been specifically for him I think was a shirt that read "May the Horse Be With You." Can't remember who claimed that one. The open gifts are being passed around the circle. I'm busy empathizing with Anne when Phyllis leans over from her seat next to me, and speaks loudly enough for the rest of the party to hear if they should like, which of course they would—it's Ellensburg.

"So, Jonathan...how's J-Bird?"

My mother and Karyn glance to one another, a look of amusement brewing.

"Um...she's good. We actually broke up about a month ago, but things are fine."

"Oh no...she was such a sweetheart. I really liked her."

"Me too. It just wasn't the right time for me."

All eyes are off the presents and on this conversation.

"Well, you'll find that special someone soon."

"Yeah, I think I'm just going to take it easy for a while. I still think I'm a little too young to get married."

Recoil. Shit. You just accidentally bashed her middle son and one of your besties. Recover quickly.

"But Rusty and Krissy are great and obviously love each other. It's just for me, there are still some things I want to do before settling down."

Phyllis doesn't miss a beat.

"I just love these parties. Your mother is so great at getting these things together. It's just such fun to see you boys back together."

"Yup. Yup. Oh, here comes another present."

I accept the passed baby blue galoshes with random horses about them, and quickly hand them off to Phyllis. I catch a smile from Casey in what has to be thanks for taking some attention off him.

"Excuse me."

I rise from my chair and quickly escape to the kitchen where Karyn is refilling her wine glass.

"So you and J-Bird are still broken up?"

"Wherever could you get that idea?"

Karyn takes a sip from her merlot while I uncap another beer, and lean against the counter.

"I think the whole party has that idea."

"Oh, that was fun, wasn't it?"

"You know what's the hardest part of breaking up? Letting people down. Not only the person who you're dumping, but everyone else who's met her and loved her. You know who I felt worst for? My mom. J-Bird was the closest thing to a daughter she's ever had. A nurse to boot. Those two would talk for hours about nursing. I think my mom is still...e-mailing with her."

"You know J-Bird is the only one you've brought home that Alice has approved of."

"I know. I know."

"Oh, Jon. You're life is just so entertaining. It's always fun to hear what you're doing, and especially who you're dating."

"Sometimes I wish it was just boring. Boring is OK sometimes. Boring but with a girl."

"Just one girl?"

"That's what I'm trying to figure out."

The party has filtered. Stos and I are lying on the couches downstairs, watching Sportscenter together for the thousandth time.

Vibration. Text from Breezy. Two days later and right on time.

"*I'm busy busy busy. How r u?*"

"*Good. In the Burg.*"

"Who's that?"

"This nineteen-year-old. I think I just need to give up on this one."

"That's pretty young."

Vibration.

"Having fun?"

"Yup, what r u up to tomorrow night?"

"I miss ESPN Deportes. All that aired was soccer."

Vibration.

"Nothing."

"I'll call you tomorrow when I'm back."

Vibration.

"Roger that."

"You see, that's what I'm fucking talking about. This chick is so cool. Who says shit like this? *'Roger that?'* No one. Ugh, why does she got to be nineteen and want nothing to do with me?"

"Sounds like you might be getting the dodge for the first time in a while."

"Maybe she really is as busy as she says she is..."

Nope.

"You know what she's doing? She's doing what I do. String it along with just enough contact to keep the other interested until you get bored, and then cut it off. She's good."

Stos adjusts the pillow behind his head.

"She's still no Panamanian."

DECEMBER 31ST / 2006 / SEATTLE

Stumbling, I climb the basement stairs leaving the flip cup game behind, but with a full beer. Leslie has put on her party mix. Justin Timberlake is currently pumping throughout the house. J-Bird's in the living room by the futon talking with Matt and Erin, and all three look drunk. Word has it Erin just broke up with her boyfriend. Go Matty. They're already drinking champagne. Yikes—It's 11:30.

The 007 theme really worked out for the best. The girls get to dress up in cocktail dresses while the boys get to do whatever they want as long as it's black. Bond probably wouldn't approve of the attire, and he definitely wouldn't approve the quality of alcohol. I bump into Evan on my way to J-Bird.

"Meyer, thanks for inviting us, man."

"No worries, Ev. Nice tuxedo tee. You guys are real d-bags."

"If you're not d-bagging you're not trying, right?"

"Who says that?"

"Nobody says that."

"That's what I thought, glad you're having a good time. Seriously though, thank J-Bird...it's her place."

"Will do."

I continue on my route, dodging through the eclectic mixture of my Gonzaga people and J-Bird's UW friends. When did all these people show up? The Gonzaga kids are sticking together as usual because why would you want to meet new people? The majority of decorations have already fallen or been pulled down.

"Hey, sexy."

"Hey there, yourself."

"So are you ready to leave California and move to Seattle yet?"

"This trip has been very inspiring."

"It's not over yet. I see you've met Erin."

"Did you know she's going to Thailand tomorrow?"

"I did not. Erin, that's quite the adventure."

"I'm going with Chris. He's picking me up in the morning."

"Like Chris, your..."

J-Bird grabs my crotch for whatever reason to shut me up, and pulls herself up to my ear. I turn with her away from Matt and Erin. There groping each other and hardly notice. I guess everyone is wasted.

"I don't think it's the best time to bring up the fact that she's going to Thailand with her ex-boyfriend when they're getting to know each other so well."

"Is this how you're going to get my attention at parties now?"

"Yeah, what do you think?"

"I think I like it."

"Let's go upstairs."

"But it's," I check my cell, "almost midnight."

"I want to get you before it's too late."

"Good point."

I grab J-Bird's hand and kiss the top of it.

"Matty, we'll see you later. Happy countdown. Hope you're lucky enough to find someone to kiss."

"I love you."

"I love you too."

J-Bird and I slide back through the living room, past the basement door, and clumsily climb the stairs to her bedroom. The crowd is too drunk to notice. Surprisingly, no one else is upstairs.

I shut J-Bird's bedroom door and we instantly come together, kissing and grabbing at each other's clothes. The light never turns on. I lift off her black dress and throw it onto the hardwood floor among her laundry. J-Bird lifts herself up into my arms, wrapping her legs above my hips for leverage, and begins unbuttoning my black shirt while I slide down my pants and step out of them. Our artificial smells have worn off, leaving only our skin's natural scent we're so familiar with now. I throw J-Bird on the bed, take off my boxers and socks, and jump on top of her. The board beneath the bed frame breaks. That's the third this month. She flips my hips and hurriedly goes down on me. Lying back, I listen as the countdown begins downstairs.

"I want my kiss."

J-Bird looks up, "Oh you'll get it."

(ten minutes later)

We entangle one another in a hot mess of skin and sweat. Our strong, pulsating hearts quickly separate our chests, and then bring us back together. J-Bird asks what I was doing last year for New Year's.

"The Gonzaga group got together at a friend's house. Wasn't that great." I press my chin down to look at J-Bird, "I'm pretty sure Lyndsay invited you and Leslie."

She says she doesn't remember, but I know she does. Not worth the words.

"Oh, um, I feel sick."

"Like pukey sick?" I inquire.

"I think so, but I never puke till the morning."

"Trust me, getting it all out before going to bed is the way to go."

"But I don't want to go all the way downstairs."

"That's fine, you can puke out Leslie's window."

"Leslie's window?"

"Yeah, I piss out it all the time when she's not in there."

J-Bird lifts her head from my chest. Just that she's considering this option means she's still drunk.

"OK."

We get out of bed. I find my boxers and slide them on while J-Bird tracks down a bra and some gym shorts. Leslie's room is directly across the hall. We open the bedroom door and the stairwell light is still on, forcing us to squint. I hear a panting noise to my right in the upstairs office. I look to find Matt and Erin very much enjoying each other's company.

"Hey, Matt."

"Hey, Jon."

"Doesn't that hurt your knees?"

"A little."

 J-Bird taps my shoulder.

"Jon! Puke."

"All right, dude, I'll see you in the morning."

I follow J-Bird into Leslie's room and run to the window. It's already open, letting the crisp now January air in. We both poke our heads out the window, taking in the height. Voices can be heard from the front of the house.

"All right, you ready?"

"Uh uh."

J-Bird begins gagging, but nothing's coming up. To try to start the process, I stick my index and middle finger down my own throat to initiate vomiting. It works. I go through four regurgitations before drying up, and spit the excess mucus from my mouth. I had hoped my own vomiting would've sparked her gag reflex, but then again she's a nurse and sees much worse on a daily basis. Blood is her weakness. J-Bird is continuing to gag, but nothing is coming out.

"All right, keep your mouth open. Is it OK if I try something?"

"Yeah."

"OK. Here we go."

I wipe the same two fingers I just used on my boxers, put them in J-Bird's mouth, and press down on the back of her tongue. Her gagging becomes more violent, and she spasms giving me enough time to pull my fingers out before she begins vomiting. I grab her hair while she continuously chucks out Leslie's window. Smiling, not from amusement, but of happiness for finally being able to help her in some way, I switch hands so my right is holding her hair, and softly stroke her bare back. Goosebumps rise. J-Bird purges her last stomach full, and slouches on the floor. I strong arm the window back into its closed position for good, slide down beside her, wrap my right arm around her, and sprawl my legs out.

"Feel better?"

"Much better. Thanks. I would've never thought to puke out Leslie's window."

"That's why you need a man like me around. Always thinking."

"Too much."

"I think people are gone. Wanna brush some teeth?"

"Yeah."

"Me too."

We lean against Leslie's bed.

"Were Matt and Erin fucking in the office?"

"I think they still are."

"That's going to be fun in the morning when Chris picks her up."

"Yup..."

"I love you."

Chuckle.

"I love you too."

Pick up the phone. Pick up the phone. Don't make me have to leave another message.

"Hello."

"Breezy?"

"Hey, Jon."

"So what do you got going tonight?"

"Nothing. Let's do something."

"That's the spirit. OK. I got *An Inconvenient Truth* and an itch for Cheesecake Factory. How's an educational movie and some dessert sound?"

"Sounds great. The cheesecake will help us feel better about how we treat our planet."

"Exactly. Pick you up in an hour?"

"Sure."

"Cool, see you then."

I shower and rub just in case anything should happen tonight. Always need the extra stamina just in case. The mustache is looking more like part of a mass beard with the weeks' worth of growth I have going, saving Breezy and myself a little embarrassment tonight. I'll clean it up tomorrow before basketball with the boys so Gee doesn't get on my ass. I throw on some jeans and the white short-sleeve button-up.

I pull the military-style hat Matt gave me during the Vegas trip nice and low, tucking in my ears on the side. The rain is slamming the roof outside my window.

I'm waiting in the rain when Breezy runs from her building with a used newspaper over her head. She's wearing a standard rain jacket, jeans, and those blue converse shoes. I love a girl without a ton of shoes. I open the passenger side door as she approaches, shutting it once she's inside. I'm wet, but I don't mind. For some reason it feels good tonight. I walk around the front of the running Element, climb inside and shut the door.

"Evening."

"How are you, other than wet?"

"Huh? Oh, great. Nothing like a weekend in Ellensburg to get your head right. You?"

"Not bad. I have some midterms this week, so I'm a little stressed."

"Well that's what chocolate's for."

The rain is lighter downtown. Streets disappear and are replaced with reflections from the city's lights. Parking is easy to find. We hustle from car to restaurant, amused by the weather. It's late so there's no line at the takeout counter.

"What are you feeling like?"

"You said, '*chocolate*' and I haven't stopped thinking about it since."

"Fair enough. I think I'm going to go with the raspberry. That looks too good."

The women at the counter must have heard our conversation because when I step to offer our requests the order is already being prepped.

"That will be fifteen dollars."

I pay and handle the large plastic bag that comes over the counter.

"That was easy. Let's go."

We walk to the revolving door, which gets sped up by a gentleman coming into the restaurant. Breezy doesn't see him and enters into the cycle without adjusting to the acceleration. The back section bumps into her and pops her forward against the front pane of glass. Breezy's knees bend but she doesn't go down, and slowly slides out of the space that's open to the street. When I get through, she's lying on the damp sidewalk, laughing uncontrollably.

"Holy shit. Are you OK?"

"Yeah, yeah. I can't believe I just did that."

I lightly grab Breezy's elbow and help her up. She's still laughing.

"You'll soon find out that I'm, well, you just found out that I'm an accident-prone person."

"No need to apologize. You're looking at a twelve-year-old in a twenty-four-year-old's frame. I haven't had control of this body in years. Sure you're OK? We can just sit here and eat these things if you really want to."

"No, no. Let's go before anything else happens."

Breezy's back up and we begin walking to the car. The Element is parked in a valet spot for Union Square

Grill. The only thing I got from that job was knowledge of a couple of sneaky parking spaces downtown. Focus on her. Eye contact. Still smiling, Breezy looks up to meet my eyes.

"You really don't have to feel embarrassed about falling down. I pretty much led Gonzaga every year in ice slips and..." my crotch runs into something that initially gives, and then shoots me back stumbling. On my third step my right ankle rolls and I collapse to the wet pavement, tumbling to the ground in a heap. Classic. The swelling is already starting in my ankle while my ego quickly deflates. Breezy's covering her laugh with a hand.

"So what was it? What did I hit?"

"A parking sign."

"Perfect. When did parking signs become half the size? I think the cheesecakes are OK."

"Fuck the cheesecakes. Are you OK?"

"No...yes...I don't know. Don't talk about the cheesecakes like that. Can you come take the bag so I can stand up?"

"Oh yeah."

Smirking, Breezy rushes over and takes the cheesecakes out of my right hand. She has a nice smile. Looking up at the skyscrapers, I put my hands on my chest and begin laughing. Lying down feels good, even with the wetness.

"I don't think it's safe to get in the car with me. You should probably walk home."

"Get up. I'm not eating this cheesecake alone. That would be more depressing than what just happened to you."

"Ouch. OK, enough self-pity. Here we go."

I stand up and brush off what I can. Unfortunately, moisture doesn't exactly vanish with the swipe of a hand. We both half limp to the Element nursing our respective injuries, and escape the treachery of downtown.

For the first time, I park and leave the Element outside of Breezy's. Inside her complex is eerily similar to the apartments at Gonzaga. I shouldn't be here. Everything about this place yells college. The unexciting carpet. Gray walls. Well lit. Sterile.

Breezy keys us into her unit that she shares with three other girls, but of course there are only two bedrooms. Fuck me. There's a mattress in the center of the common area, just below the foot of the couch.

"What's up with mattress?"

"Sometimes Robin and I, she's my roommate, just need to get away from each other."

Or one of you is hooking up with somebody, but that's just what guys would do. Don't judge. Open mind. New experiences. More like old, new experiences.

"I'll work the cake out. You wanna get the movie going? You'd probably have better luck with the DVD than me."

"Sure."

I slop chunks of the each cake onto plates, and pour a couple of glasses of tap water for good measure. Breezy's got the movie ready prepped, and has positioned herself on the couch. After handing her some chocolate cake, my raspberry and I plop a safe, but not too far distance from Breezy.

"Ready?"

"Let's get educated."

Half my cake rests on the couch between Breezy and me. I'm full, and suffering the effects of a sugar crash without receiving the high first. Gore is making me feel more and more guilty. I need to ride my bike more. I'm hoping Big Al will come out and say something like, *"If you really want to make a difference, just put Jon Meyer out of his misery and start making out with him because he sure as hell won't make a move because he feels real awkward about this age situation, and is scared to even touch you,"* but am pretty sure he's going to stick to the environment, and not my lack of initiative. Let's break down the situation. She's at least a half cushion away with picked-at cheesecake blocking direct contact. Let's clear that cheesecake.

"Done with your cake?"

"Yeah, thanks."

"No worries."

I grab both our plates and haul them to the kitchen, refrigerating them with saran wrap. Deciding to take advantage of the mattress, I occupy the space just to the right of her legs, and lean against the couch. At this point, I have full access to her feet should I gain enough courage to start a foot massage, or she can initiate a little head massage on me. Fuck Gore, you are not helping sexy time. Why can't we be watching *The Notebook*? Girls love that movie.

Breezy shifts back up on the couch, leaving her right leg resting against my shoulder. Did she sense me thinking about *The Notebook*? What's this mean? Maybe she does want a foot massage. I should be the one getting a foot worked on after the downtown debacle. OK, game plan. You have a free arm that is fully capable of doing a wrap-around calf rub. That could be too much, and what if she pulls away? You might as well leave at that point. Where's the always available blanket for us to share? I need a blanket to share. This is hopeless. This apartment, other than the random mattress I'm sitting on, is completely hookup proof. I'm fighting a lost cause, and I was insensible to it to begin with! She's nineteen! She has every SPU soccer douche asking her out. At this point in her life, soccer players are way more attractive than twenty-four-year-old sales reps who do nothing all day. You are that creepy out-of-college guy you used to hate. I want to be that soccer douche. Whoever said chicks like older guys because they're more sexually experienced was lying. Maybe I should tell her I'm very sexually experienced. That's kind of true. I got tricks I could show her.

"*And look at this graph, folks. When observing Seat-tle and the likes of Jon Meyer, they have no chance of survival on their current course. It's time to buck up, or get out of the apartment.*"

It's over. Both the movie and my chances. I stand up and head for the door. Breezy, bless her heart, fol-lows me.

"So good luck with your midterms."

"Thanks, and thanks for the movie and cake. It was really good."

Which one?

"No problem. Well, you're the busy one, so call when you got some free time. I'm around for a while before my next business trip."

Yes, make yourself sound important.

"OK. See ya, Jon."

"See ya."

I don't even attempt a hug, let alone a kiss on the cheek, and exit stage left. If I go in for the kiss and get the hug, that throws me into instant friend zone with no way out. Best just let this one stir. She must have liked the fall down thing. Chicks dig that stuff. If she calls within two weeks, I'm still in it. Yikes.

For some reason I'm staring at Laura brown, petit little blonde, and she's staring right back. Jack and Dan's is hopping with graduation around the corner, and everyone's chosen J and D's over the Bulldog tonight. I'm sitting at the round table in the front of the bar by the entrance with Larky, Jack, and Matt. We opted for pitchers over waiting for individual drinks at the bar. I'm still a little full from the pre-funk second Old English forty. This late in the year, J and D's is a mad house. Outkast is blaring over the crowd noise.

"Where's Shawnee?"

"She and Angie are near the back."

"Why aren't you two with them?"

"What kind of question is that, Larky?"

"A fair one."

"That's true."

Matt drops his head in disappointment.

"Who you staring at, Jon?"

"Laura Brown of all people. I've never said more than five sentences to her, and we are just eye-fucking the shit out of each other right now. She doesn't usually curl her hair like that, does she?"

"I love a good eye fuck."

"Well, boys, it's the end of the year, and what do we say?"

"Do you have a job?"

"No."

"Do you have herpes?"

"Close. We say *no regrets*."

"What's that supposed to mean?"

"It means I'm going to try to hook up with Laura Brown tonight."

"But what about Angie?"

"What about her?"

"The letter?"

"Matt, how do you know about that?"

"Do you really have to ask?"

"You're right. Fuck it. Angie and I have had our chances the last month though, and nothing's happened. I'm not spending my last days in Spokane waiting for Angie."

"A man on a mission."

"That's right, Larky."

"But what about us? What about the boys?"

"Lark, I've lived across the hall from you for the last two years. If you've wanted to hook up you've had plenty of chances to sneak into my room."

"You cut straight to the heart."

"All right, here we go."

Laura and I walk past the boys and out of Jack and Dan's. I refrain from looking at them from fear of breaking out in a dance. The Triangle is bustling with familiar faces jumping bar to bar. I nod to Sherm across the street who's working the hot dog stand. He'd definitely give me one, but that would destroy my breath. I think we're going to her place too, so no toothbrush. Shit.

"I like what you did with your hair tonight."

"Thanks."

Footsteps are approaching quickly from behind. Laura and I turn to see Shawnee bounding up the sidewalk.

"Jon! Jon. I need to talk to you."

"I'm a little busy, Shawnee. Not a good time."

"Just for a second."

"Sorry, Laura. Do you mind?"

"No problem."

"Thanks."

Laura waits by the crosswalk while Shawnee and I walk back in front of Jack and Dan's. Over her shoulder I can see Matt giving two thumbs-up inside the bar.

"Angie wants you tonight. She wants to hook up with you tonight!"

"Oh, she just decided this, did she?"

"Yeah, so...are you going to come back inside?"

"No. Obviously, I have other plans. Thanks for making things really awkward though. Tell Angie to give me a day's notice next time so I can clear my schedule, please."

"It might not happen again, Jon."

"I'll take the risk. Thanks, Shawnee."

I turn and walk back to Laura, catching a glimpse of Matt dropping his arms in disappointment. Not tonight, buddy.

With no toothbrush, I just squirt some toothpaste in my mouth and slosh it around. Laura's in bed by the time I'm done in the bathroom. The lights are already off. I strip down to my boxers and slide between the sheets. She moves over to apparently give me the room I need, when all I really want her to do is crawl on top of me and take control because I'm so mind-fucked I can't make the first move. Goddamnit, Shawnee. Why did you have to come out of Jack and Dan's?

Motionless, we fall asleep, backs to each other.

"So am I going to get to meet this girl?"

Goob and I continue down Roosevelt in the Element, trying to get to the bar early enough to score some seats. I'm buzzing from the oil can of Foster's I drank on the back nine at Jackson, and it's making more and more sense that A-bomb would want to come out.

"Ya know, Goob, let's give her a call."

I Bring up her text from the other day, and press the talk button on my phone.

"Jessica's going to love this. She always gives you shit about the girls you're messing around with. Robbie is going to be there tonight too."

"Good, someone else for her to talk at. I like him though, good guy."

Shit. The machine.

"Hey, A-bomb, it's Jon. Just calling to see if you wanted to listen to some bluegrass band at Pies and Pints tonight? I'm meeting some Ellensburg people there. Shouldn't last more than a couple of hours. Let me know."

"No answer?"

"No answer."

"So who's this chick?"

"This girl I met a couple of summers ago. She found me on MySpace last year and we hung out a couple of times, but that didn't sit well with J-Bird, so I stopped talking to her."

"Hung out? Really?"

"Nothing ever happened. Take it easy."

After multiple dinners eaten, Goob rightfully feels loyalty to J-Bird.

"So I called her about a month ago."

"Because you and J-Bird broke up."

"More or less. She's a cool girl though. I'm not going to go dating her or anything, but I'll watch a movie now and then."

"And what do you think she thinks about this?"

"I don't know; we've never talked about it."

"So you guys just basically just watch movies and have sex?"

"Um...correct."

"A world I have no idea about."

"A world I used to enjoy. Now I'm not so sure."

They're aren't any spots in front of the bar, so I take the next left and park in front of a house on the nearest side street. Stepping out the car, I feel my phone vibrate. It's A-bomb.

"Hey."

"Hey, are you guys at the bar yet?"

"Just pulling up."

"OK, I just got off work. I'll be there in thirty minutes."

"Do you know where Pies and Pints is?"

"On Sixty-fifth, right?"

"Yeah, good girl."

"See you soon."

"OK."

I jog across Sixty-fifth and catch up with Goob who's standing next to the entrance. Twangs are vibrating through the walls of the bar.

"She coming?"

"Yeah."

"You having sex with her tonight?"

"Yeah."

"You're a dick."

"I know."

We enter the bar and instantly the volume is turned up. The bluegrass band is made up of a couple of Whitworth guys that Goob and Jessica know. They're pretty good even though I think they have only about eight songs in their repertoire. The fiddle player is really on point tonight. Jessica waves her hand from a booth in the back of the bar. Good thing she got here before we did because the place is packed. Hipsters fill the tables and watch the band pass solos back and forth. For not much of a stage show, they sure are mesmerizing.

"I think it would be best if we didn't bring up the fact that Jessica and me messed around in high school in front of Robbie."

"Sounds good."

"Really, Goob, don't just say that and then start talking about shit like you always do."

"I will not discuss how you used to go over to Jessica's in the middle of day to get hand jobs."

"For a good Christian, you can be a dick sometimes."

Goob and I slide into the booth, leaving Jessica as the only one facing the band back at that front of the bar. Her hair is darkly shaped around her face, and is contrasted by her white shirt. She's always been a small package, but perfectly proportional. I'm sure she's wearing some tweed pants with sneakers under the table.

"Hey, fellas."

"Jessica, always a pleasure."

"It's been awhile, Jon. Nice stache. I think the last time we talked you and J-Bird had just broken up. How are you?"

"He's fine. Has a girl on the way."

"You're a dick. You're a dick, man."

"Jon, Jon...moving on so quickly. I don't know if that's healthy."

"I'm fine. I'm exercising my rights as a single man. Where's Robbie?"

"Oh, way to change the subject. He's on his way. Finishing up with his youth group."

I motion to the waitress for two beers. I owe Goob from golf.

"Looks like you're wheeling tonight again, Glas. When we going to find you a girl?"

"I got girls. They just have boyfriends that they haven't left yet."

"Still going with that story, huh?"

"You know it."

"Glas, I can't even think of a type for you. I'm trying to think of girls I know to set you up with, and nothing is coming to mind."

The beers arrive.

"Drink up, Glas. Who knows, maybe you'll find a wifey in here tonight."

"She better like the Seahawks."

"I think you might have to expand your criterion. Then again, you've always been in love with Jessica. She would work."

"Goob had his shot with me and blew it. I need a man who's not afraid to make the move."

"She's right. I need to work on my courage."

"Well, drink up. That always helps."

I check the door for the umpteenth time, and finally see A-bomb walking through. She's noticeably shaken by the volume being produced by the band. I wave my hand because the booth is so high my head is barely visible. She looks good tonight. Funky khakis and a little jean jacket.

"Get out, Goob."

"Why?"

"Because I want her on the inside so I can talk to her."

"But you guys don't talk. You just watch movies and fuck."

"Goob!"

"Thank you, Jessica. That was a rude thing to say. Clean your mouth up."

"Clean your life up."

"I'm working on it."

A-bomb approaches the booth and saddles up cautiously, not knowing anyone but me.

"Hey, you look great. This is Goob and Jessica. Two friends from Ellensburg who are making it in the big city as well."

"A pleasure to meet you two."

"Nice to meet you too. Have a seat next to me."

Uh oh. Jessica is already trying to make friends. Nothing good can come of this. She's been a confidant through the years and knows secrets that could ruin me should they get out to the wrong party. She liked J-Bird and that's the only reason she kept quiet about our misdeeds. If A-bomb gets off on the wrong foot, I'm ruined. I dent my beer. A-bomb motions to a waitress and orders a gin and tonic.

"So what do you do, A-bomb?"

"I work at Pagliaccis. Sorry I was late, I had to wash the smell of pizza off me."

"That's fine, and you go to school?"

"I finished at UW in accounting last spring, and am still working at Pagliaccis. It's so frustrating trying to find the right job."

"Even if you know what you want to do, I can't think of anyone who is actually doing it."

"The job market is just so saturated and people are working longer. Greatest generation, my ass."

"That's our parents you're talking about, Jessica."

"And..."

"And...good point. So I take it you're still a nanny?"

"Yup. That whole San Francisco work study thing didn't exactly work out."

"Seattle would've missed you."

"It brought me back."

Our waitress brings A-bomb another gin and tonic. That should be enough for her. Goob looks disgusted with his beer, and looks set on ordering a cocktail. The band announces that they'll be playing their last song because the fiddle player broke his second string of the night. I didn't notice the first one. My buzz is pacing itself after another Mac and Jack's. Goob's taking a piss and wants to leave. Robbie emerges from the crowd, and sits next to his girl. They talk amongst each other in the corner of the booth, so I lean across the table to A-bomb.

"I have to take Goob back to my apartment for his car, but I'd like to come over tonight."

"Sounds good."

"Then I'll see you later. I'll bring some movie options."

"OK."

Glaser and I part at the Watermarke with a mini-lecture on how I'm living my life. He really liked J-Bird. All the dinners we invited him over for didn't hurt her reputation. She's a good cook.

I drive the route to A-bomb's that's becoming oddly familiar. My legs are achy from the golf and lack of water. Traffic is light as usual. Her driveway is empty, so instead of flipping a bitch to park alongside the curb, I take the vacant spot. Her roommates must be gone.

After a couple of knocks, A-bomb unlatches the door and lets me in. She's changed into black sweats and an olive tank top that disappears into her skin.

"So what movies did you bring?"

Shit.

"Shit. I forgot them. Sorry."

"That's all right, I'm pretty tired anyways. I guess we'll just have to go to bed?"

"Sounds good. I'm going to grab some water. You want any?"

"I'll just have some of yours."

A-bomb goes into the bathroom and begins brushing her teeth. I really like her house. Hardwood floors. Generous bedrooms. Well-designed kitchen with new appliances. I pull a pint glass out of a kitchen cupboard, and fill it with ice and water from the refrigerator. I need to piss but A-bomb's still in the bathroom. I move to her room, place the water on the bedside table, and strip down to my boxers. The glow from a streetlight is enough to illuminate her room with an orange tint. A light breeze is coming in from a cracked window, creating a comfortable temperature for sleeping. I hop under the comforter.

The buzzing from A-bomb's Sonicare stops and is directly followed by the click of the light switch. The bathroom door creaks and I leave the comforts of the bed for a bathroom trip. We meet at the door.

"Thanks."

Even after drinking some water, my mouth still tastes like beer. I squeeze some toothpaste onto my index finger, and grind it around my mouth. Her sink is small so it's quite the task bending down and getting my head low enough to get some tap water for rinsing. I slosh the water around, hopefully releasing most of the sticky blue substance in my mouth.

A-bomb's in bed when I return from the bathroom. She has the comforter pulled all the way to her chin. I stand in the doorway.

"Any room in there for me?"

"Maybe."

I jump to the inside of the bed, solidifying a wall sleeping position for the night. Lying flat, pressure built up from golfing releases from my legs and knees. A-bomb's body heat has warmed the bed, so much so that I apply the comforter to only the lower half of my body. A-bomb squirms over and shapes her body into my torso. As before, I slide my arm under her neck and hook her just above the hip. My forearm is pushing up her already very visible breasts, and my body takes an interest. She feels this and does a slow grind against my torso, making me instantly hard.

A-bomb rolls over and we begin to kiss, our heads slightly angled by our pillows. This is awkward. I push off on my right arm and take the upper position. She still must be a little drunk because she's being more forceful with the tongue than usual. In unison, we slide hands under each other's waistline. She's wet. A-bomb shifts her weight and moves herself into the top position, still keeping her right hand clamped around me. She raises her left hand to my shoulder for support, and she begins lightly kissing my chest. Her head slowly moves down my torso. She must be on her period again. Her lips are moist as she takes me in. I flex my torso in an effort to minimize the amount time before climax. A-bomb's straddling my taut right quad, leaving my left leg stiff, toes pointed straight up in exertion. My sacrifice isn't nearly as large as hers, but nonetheless, I'm dedicated to the act as well. With all the force, my left calf explodes in a knot of pain.

"Shit Fuck!"

A-bomb pops her head up.

"Everything OK?"

Tight lipped, "Yup. Just fine. You're doing great."

I jerk up on my elbows to relieve some of the pressure, but the movement just squeezes the muscle tighter. My mind drifts from the moment. A fucking cramp? Really? I pull myself up a bit and give A-bomb the thumbs-up with a forced smile. Her head goes back down. I don't deserve her dedication. Just relax the leg. You can do this. My mind is so off track, that if I don't focus poor A-bomb will be down there for twenty minutes. I search my brain for banked memories of guaranteed arousal, and along comes J-Bird. The old go-to. We're having sex in my bed and she's on top, smiling down at me. Her hands are planted on my chest, balancing her as I slowly rotate my hips underneath her. My right hand locks into her hip while my left moves up her stomach to her beautiful right breast, grazing the little birthmark underneath. We move together slowly, in perfect rhythm with each other.

Back with A-bomb, I cum, releasing pressure from all areas of my body. Muscle release and afterglow takes me over. A-bomb takes it in and kisses her way back up my chest. I exhale deeply and meet A-bomb's lips.

"That was scary there for a second."

"Whew, I'm just fine. Really fine." My head flops back to the pillow. "It's you who needs to work on your schedule so we can get you taken care of as well."

"The next movie."

"Yeah, the next movie."

JUNE 18TH / 2006 / SEATTLE

I'm checking fantasy baseball when my phone rings. J-Bird and Jeff are watching TV. Moopy's still moving some swords or something into his room. It's Angie.

"What up?"

"Ready for that walk."

Shit. I totally forgot.

"Um, yeah. When did you want to go?"

"I'm working at the restaurant tonight for Liz, so right now is probably the best time."

How's this going to work?

"Should I come get you?"

"Yeah, see you in a few."

I hang up and swivel back to J-Bird. She's turned from the TV, and is looking at me.

"Who was that?"

"Angie. I forgot a couple of days ago I told her I'd go on a walk today. I'm sorry, but I have to do this. I haven't seen her in a month."

"Well how long is it going to take?"

"Shouldn't be more than hour. Sorry."

J-Bird turns back to the TV, obviously not happy about the idea of me spending time with Angie. Why can't they just be friends?

The walking trail is packed as expected. Half of Seattle must be rollerblading around Greenlake. Sun brings everyone out. Angie and I come upon the west end swimming area where hundreds of kids are running about in the early summer sun while parents read and socialize.

"Can we sit down here?"

"Sure. Is the small talk over?"

We squat on an open patch of grass among the adults.

"Afraid so. I wanted to talk to you about our friendship, or what's left of it, which I don't think is much. I haven't seen you in forever, and to me you're making no effort of sustaining it. Would you agree?"

Pause. Think. Yes.

Uneasily, I begin, "Yeah, I would. J-Bird does take up most of my time along with working two jobs, but I haven't been as good to you girls, you specifically, as I used to. I see that. But she's my girlfriend, Angie, and a pretty serious one at that. At least more serious than I've ever been before. I don't mean to take this conversation off my inefficiencies, but you haven't exactly made an effort to get to know her either. Other than Lyndsay, I would consider you my closest girl friend, and to have you not like J-Bird influences my decision making."

Angie takes that one in.

"I'll be honest, I was jealous in the beginning. Probably still am a little. You're, you were, our guy, Jon. The guy we depended on. Remember sitting in the booth, everyone bullshitting about how hard it's been since graduating?"

"Yeah, I miss that, but I just can't give you the time I used to. J-Bird gets that time now. I had to leave her at the new apartment to come here. And the booth is gone, Angie. It's harder to keep in touch when you guys don't live right up the street anymore."

"Well anything more than you're giving now would be nice."

"I'll try. Honestly, it's been on my mind. I just, I love her, Angie. She's the first girl I can say that about. I actually enjoy spending time with her, unlike most of my girlfriends in the past where I spent the least amount of time with them in hopes of keeping demand up."

"Demand?"

I've said too much.

"Yeah, you know...basic supply and demand. The more time I spend with a girl the less I want to see her."

Angie takes that one in too.

"When are you going to stop seeing life like running a business?"

"You know I can't help it. Seriously though, I'll make an effort if you make an effort. J-Bird wants to get to know you. She's heard all the stories and knows what we've been through, understands that we're close. It would mean a lot to me if you two became friends so we could all hang out."

Angie nods her head. I'm sure she expected that request to come out of this conversation as well.

"Deal."

"Fantastic."

J-Bird's sitting in the same spot when I get back to the apartment. According to her, Jeff left for Jacki's. Moopy is building his desk. She wants to know if we can go up on the roof.

"Sure."

J-Bird stands up and I follow her out the apartment door. Roofside, the temperature has cooled since I left Greenlake, and a summer zephyr is picking up. The downtown buildings are orange with the setting sun's reflection. The roof's beige patio furniture is strewn about from a party last night. We grab a couple of chairs, and move them together. Since it was her request, I await conversation. J-Bird doesn't wait long.

"I just have to come out and ask—are you cheating on me?"

Here we go...

"No. No. And no. J-Bird, why would you think that?"

"Because you just left in the middle of the day to go hang out with Angie."

"I told you, I had promised her that we'd hang out this weekend, and I totally forgot. You want to know what we talked about? How I haven't been a good friend to her because I've been spending all my time with you. That's kind of true, but I defended myself... defended us."

"She just makes me uncomfortable, and I don't trust her. It's obvious she still likes, maybe even loves you, and I know you say that you haven't seen her in a month but I don't know what you're really doing with your free time."

"Love? I told you before, if something was going to happen between me and Angie it already would have. Nothing happened in college, and New Year's was the final straw. After that, I gave up on anything serious with her. Nothing is going on. When I'm with you, I'm only with you."

"OK."

"I need you to trust me, J-Bird. If I don't have that then I'm going to be second-guessing everything I do and who I hang out with. I don't think I could handle that."

J-Bird looks back at the city, her body noticeably more relaxed.

"It's just that, OK, I'm going to tell you something."

"I'm listening."

"My dad cheated...is probably still cheating on my mom."

Jesus.

"He had been helping this woman who was doing some work for him at the warehouse, and it turned into something more. Since he was gone all the time anyways for work, nothing was really out of the ordinary. After time, someone dropped off an anonymous note under our door for my mom saying he was seeing this woman. I think my mom kind of assumed something was going on already, but once it was verified she was distraught."

I grab for J-Bird's legs, place them in my lap, and gently stroke her calves.

"When did you find out about this?"

"I was fifteen. Old enough to understand what was happening. Krista still doesn't really know. Even though my mom half knew, she still felt stupid and duped." J-Bird looks into my eyes. "I don't want to feel that way, Jon. I don't want to be the only one who doesn't know something you're doing. I don't want to feel like I'm the only one on the outside."

"J-Bird, I will never cheat on you. I care too much about you and us to do anything like that. You know I hate disappointing people, and doing something like that would completely kill us. I've had opportunities in the past, twice, to cheat and I never have."

"When?"

"Once in college, and the other time was in high school. Both good offers, but I couldn't do it. It's not in me. I'm sorry about Angie. She is a fairly controlling person and usually gets what she wants, but I told her I'm with you and my commitment, right now, is to you. I also told her that the only way we're going to be able to spend more time together is if she backs off a little, and makes an effort to get to know you. Both of you have so much in common. I really think you'd get along."

"I just wish she wasn't such a bitch whenever she's around."

I lean forward and grab J-Bird's hand.

"She'll settle down. Are we OK? Do you trust me?"

"Yes."

"OK."

During the late 1980s and early '90s, the mustache became virtually extinct. Being almost exclusively worn in the mainstream by baby boomers, the mustache's reputation was tarnished by its associations within the pornographic industry and pedophilia. Throughout the '90s and into the new century, the mustache's popularity continued to dwindle, often being passed over for other facial hair styles such as the goatee and its cousins. Short of a grassroots effort to change mass opinion, it looks as though the mustache may die with the baby boomer generation.

Date night is struggling so far. The waiter at the dumpling restaurant made me look like an idiot for not knowing what to order, and now J-Bird and I are on our third theatre, trying to find a non-sold-out show of *The Departed*. Ballard is hopping. The closest parking spot to the theatre is still two blocks away. J-Bird's being a good sport. She knows I really want to see the movie, and was really just along for the dumplings.

"Cold. Cold. Cold."

"Hopefully there's not much of a line."

Once away from the Escort, I wrap my arm around her shoulder and bring her in. Every other street light is lit. Teeth are chattering. Her blue pea coat is still missing the button that accidentally ripped off a month ago. The cold deserves more than a fleece.

We arrive at the back of the line for the theater that ends where the street begins. Cars rush by to their destinations, adding an extra chill to the December night. Everyone else in line is here to see *The Departed* too—not a good sign. I follow the steam from my breath, and watch it linger with everyone else's in line just above our heads.

"That's it, folks! *The Departed* is sold out!"

Defeat is realized. Groans quickly fade as the assembly scatters for cars.

"Fuck it. To bed?"

"I, I, I can do that."

"C'mon. Let's get you back in the car."

Still wrapped in my arms, J-Bird and I leave the bright lights of Market Street for the warmth of the Escort.

"Thanks for trying. The next date night will be better."

"Yeah. Let's just get home."

"Yup."

A couple of girls are walking toward us. One's wearing a green U of O sweatshirt, and looks kind of famili... shit. It's A-bomb. You have a half block. Think quickly. Would J-Bird be more upset if you didn't introduce her now, and told her later that we walked past A-bomb, or do you run the ultimate risk and introduce her now? She'll be more pissed later on. Act surprised.

"A-bomb?"

A-bomb and who I'm assuming is a roommate stutter stop.

"Jon? Hey, how are you?"

"Fine. Cold. Just wrapping up an unsuccessful date night. What are you doing?"

"Um, well, we're getting cupcakes."

"Nice. Hey, this is my girlfriend J-Bird."

"Hi, J-Bird. I'm A-bomb and this is my roommate Claire."

Not going too bad. Might get out of here unscathed.

"Nice to meet you. Sorry, I'm a little cold."

"Yeah, we should get home. Enjoy your cupcakes."

"Will do. Good seeing you."

"You too."

The heat finally kicks on. Feeling is returning to my hands.

"Did you see the look on her face, Jon?"

J-Bird's warmed up.

"Um, I just saw A-bomb. It was dark and I wanted to get you back in the car."

"It's obvious she thought you were lying before when you told her you had a girlfriend."

"I don't think that's true."

"Girls can sense these things."

"I think you picked up something from that conversation that wasn't there. Would you rather we walked by her with me not saying anything? Not introduce you two? Keep her out there as some mystery woman?"

"No."

"OK, then. I'm trying to do the everything-open-and-honest thing here, J-Bird, and that's a step. Now you know what she looks like and what she's all about. She's about cupcakes and sweat pants."

J-Bird straightens and looks forward.

"Sweat pants can be sexy."

"I like scrubs better. How 'bout we go home, get you into some sexy scrubs, and then get you out of those scrubs."

"That sounds better than date night."

"Hey, those dumplings were the truth."

"Too bad the server was more of a man than you. Letting some other guy order for your girlfriend."

"You can take your own scrubs off with an attitude like that."

Seattle's downtown lunch crowd fills the bottom of Pacific Place in droves. Light coming through the skylight fills the four-story mall. Suit after suit lines up at Il Fornaio, waiting to consume their overpriced pasta salad or panini. Debi wanted to talk about something. She just finished showing the spring line to the Nordstrom people, and was late as usual.

"I'm sorry, Jon, but I have to let you go."

Yup. Fuck me.

"Corporate is shrinking my territory, and unless they decide to open it back up, I can't afford to keep you on anymore. It has nothing to do with you or your performance. They're just moving everything to work wear, and cutting out rec."

Think.

"Can you just let me internalize this for a second?"

"Sure."

OK. You're still due some commissions. Salary too. Shit. My face drops into my hands, and stretches on its way up.

"So where do we go from here? I need some money to keep living, Debi. Something so I can float awhile before I find another job. I've spent a fair amount of cash to get myself going with this job, and travel expenses...shit...sorry."

"I know, Jon. I'll pay you for this month and every order that got turned in before the end of the month. Also, I'll pay you for your preseason orders that had an increase of 20 percent from last year."

"Why don't I get a commission on all the orders?"

"Because I had to front for you starting out."

What the fuck? I don't remember that being the deal. Calm down.

"OK. Can I go home and think about this a bit, crunch some numbers, and then get back to you? I just need to get out of my own head for a second."

"That's fine. I'm sorry again. This had nothing to do with you. I'm more than happy to write a letter of rec or anything you need."

Exhale.

"Sure."

And that's how you get laid off.

"Breezy, I didn't expect an answer. I already had my message ready to go."

"Nope, I'm here. What's up?"

"Nothing, just wondering what you're up to this week. School's over, right?"

"Yeah, well I'm pretty busy actually. I'm moving back home tomorrow for a week, and then going on vacation with my parents."

Done. This is done.

"That sounds like fun. OK, well can I check in with you down the road?"

Reaching now a bit, aren't you?

"Sounds good, Jon. Have a nice summer."

Summer? All summer?

"Will do. Take it easy, Breezy."

"Bye."

I try to open the door to Angie's house, but it's locked. Doesn't anyone keep their doors unlocked anymore? The night is warm, hazy clouds absorbing light from the city. I rap the window three times. Thumping footsteps run to the door. Angie emerges from behind.

"Hey."

"Hey, boy."

She's in her Gonzaga sweat suit outfit, glasses, and weird fuzzy socks that J-Bird wears as well.

"Nice outfit."

"Don't mock my sexiness."

"No mocking here, just compliments."

"Bring movies?"

"You going to let me in?"

"Only if you have movies."

I pull two Blockbuster rentals from my hoodie for visual confirmation. Angie steps aside.

"Come on in."

I step into the house.

"So easy to please."

"You know me."

"Yes, I do."

"So how'd the talk with Debi go today?"

"Um...it actually got pushed back to the end of the week. She had to head to Montana for business."

"Oh, what do you think it's about?"

"You know, probably the company. Things are changing and I'm sure she has some new info or something."

"Think you're OK?"

"For now, yeah."

The Good German is boring enough for my attention to drift from the plot, and onto my self-developed predicament. What am I doing? More like, what the hell was I thinking when I kissed Angie the first time? Her hair smells nice. I move my right leg off the futon and slide up a little, putting Angie's head more on my chest than collarbone.

You've got to end it with A-bomb. Then again, she's gone along with this for a while now without wanting to have "The Talk." That's a good sign. But no chick's that cool. It doesn't feel right anyways. OK, that's it. Squash things with A-bomb. In time.

Angie wraps her left arm around my leg, and begins caressing my calf with her thumb.

So what then with J-Bird? You have to end that too. Not that anything's going on, but all thoughts of hooking up or ever dating J-Bird again have got to go. You'll never really let go unless you stop entertaining the thought that you're still going to hook up with her. She was right; maybe it should have been a clean cut. No talking. No texting. No Facebook messages. A clean sever.

Angie's head falls limply off my chest. She's asleep. I don't blame her, this movie blows. I nudge her with my knuckle. She's back.

"Hey, ready for bed? I can't follow what's happening."

"Yeah."

She grabs one of the three remotes and turns everything off.

"Am I staying over?"

"Yeah."

We straggle into her bedroom. The fan is going full blast. The window is cracked, letting not only cool air in but street noise. I like sleeping with street noise. Angie promptly shuts the window, and crawls into bed.

Standing in the middle of the dark room, I shake my hips, allowing my scrubs to fall to the floor. I peel my shirt off and carefully step over Angie to the inside of the bed. I'm hot as usual. Angie throws some comforter on me, but I keep it off my upper body. I don't want to start sweating. Angie's hand grabs my arm and lifts it over her, pulling me into her body. My nose is pressing against her check. My body warms. Air from the fan hits my face. I'm not tired. Her lips are pouting out like a middle school girl, reaching for a kiss. In one motion, I slide my left hand to her hip while pushing up on my right forearm, and begin kissing her. She engages and runs her hand through my hair.

"I like it shorter."

"That's not important now."

I press my lips harder, cracking my mouth open and pressing my tongue to meet hers. My left hand is fumbling, trying to get under her sweatshirt. Finally, I just lift the Gonzaga hoodie off, and drop it alongside the bed. How can she sleep in all these clothes? Passing headlights allow glimpses of her supple stomach. I've never seen it in person, only in pictures plastered on her fridge. Pulling down her baggy bottoms, I'm not slowed by any underwear. I kiss the inside of her legs, eventually making my way up. Angie's bare and smooth. She has no smell. Never have I come across a girl that had no smell, good or bad. She's mumbling to herself and stroking my head.

"Do you have a condom?"

"Yeah. You ready?"

"Yeah."

Grabbing my scrubs from the floor, I locate the condom in the back pocket. I rip the wrapper and roll the condom onto me, but I'm not hard enough for it to fully take. Expecting me, Angie arches her back. I plant my hands on either side of her shoulders, pull myself back on the bed, and press between her legs. Angie handles and guides me. The condom deafens her warmth. She's obviously uncomfortable, so I start slow. Nothing fancy. I raise her right leg above my shoulder.

"No—stop. OK, right there."

I back off more, bringing my knees up for a different angle. I lift Angie by the small of her back, pacing off her breathing. Her panting slows, and then stops. She's not responding to anything. This isn't going well. Stay here. Stay with her.

In an attempt to get anything going, I pick up the rhythm. Angie turns her face into the pillow. This is hopeless. Just finish. Flustered, I start to sweat. I move my sweaty right hand from underneath Angie's back to her breast, and focus on its textures. Without theatrics, I finish and collapse beside her, a touch confused.

JANUARY 22ND / 2007 / LAS VEGAS

I can't take Vegas anymore, and it's only the second day of SIA. Industry hipsters and squares alike run around the Mandalay Bay convention center, rushing to their next appointments. Endless rows of signs and glorified cardboard boxes line one after another, each with a name that if you don't recognize will probably be the next big thing. Oxygen and air conditioning are being pumped from the pipes above. Seventy five degrees outside is apparently too much to handle.

J-Bird's exploring Vegas while I finish with my last two accounts. I hope she shows for Evo so I can have a model.

"Jon, your four o'clock is here. The family owned shop in Seattle. She's waiting out front."

"Thanks, Lyndz."

Thank God Lyndsay is here. Another apathetic soul to our industry. I follow Lyndsay out front to see Nicole wandering around with her notebooks being held against her chest. Our footsteps get her attention.

"Jon?"

"Yes, are you Nicole?"

"Yup, Nicole Forrest. Nice to meet you."

She's cute. A brunette with a round face and nice smile.

"OK, so if you just follow me back, we have showroom three set up for us."

I lead her behind the walking models and rotating mannequins to the back of the Helly setup that houses the showrooms. What was supposed to have every style and color for the upcoming season, showroom three has been picked apart and I'll be lucky if I have to make the assistant run for clothes only four or five times.

"So what kind of business do you have, Nicole?"

"It's a ski shop between Queen Anne and Magnolia."

"Nice. I live in Wallingford. I can't believe I haven't noticed it before."

"It's a little shack right off Fifteenth. Easy to breeze by."

"I'll be stopping in from now on. What kind of price points are we going to be working with today?"

"Most of our customers are coming down from Queen Anne, so are ready to spend top dollar."

"Then I'll go ahead show you everything we're offering for next year."

"Sounds great."

We duck into our box of a room that's no larger than eight by ten feet. I step behind the slanted stainless steel desk, and take position in front of the two hanging racks of clothes.

"All right. I have a buyer's guide right in front of you. If you could flip to page forty-eight, I'll go ahead and start with base layer."

"And if you take a look at the details on the arm, you can tell they did a great job with this piece."

"Again, the detailing on this style is fantastic."

"They really thought about this piece when putting it together."

"Yup, those *are* little bedazzles. Good eye."

"And the details...this is my favorite piece."

When J-Bird emerges from between Salomon and Patagonia, I'm finished and sprawled on the couch in front of the booth. Compared to the other industry types running around, she looks quite bland in just jeans, a tee shirt, and Pumas. I love it. I pat my lap, inviting her on.

"How'd it go?"

"Not bad. I'm exhausted. If I say the word 'detail' one more time my head is going to explode. Is there another adjective out there to replace it?"

"I think it's a noun."

"Whatever it is, I never want to say it again. Ready for dinner?"

"Yup. Where do you want to go for the big night?"

"I was thinking we could walk back through the hotel and weigh our options."

"Love it."

J-Bird pulls me off the couch, and I throw my arm over her shoulder. My knees feel swollen.

"Lyndsay already leave?"

"Yeah, she and Leslie are getting dinner in the Luxor. It's me and you, girl. Happy one year."

"Happy one year."

We decide that Wolfgang Puck will work. I'm tired. The wine isn't helping.

"So what'd you see today?"

"I walked all the way up to Treasure Island and back. Looked at some shops. Feel like I got it in for the most part. It's concerning...the fakeness."

"Of the buildings?"

"No, the people. Everyone is here because they want to do or act like they never could where they're from. I don't think it's healthy."

"Probably better they do it here than at home?"

"Maybe, who am I to say anything? It's their life. When I'm sixty I'm sure I'll come every other weekend."

I raise my wine glass in a toasting fashion, waiting for J-Bird to meet my eyes.

"Here's to making it until sixty, and here's to us. Happy one year. It's been one of the best years of my life...and the main reason is you."

J-Bird bobs her head and smiles. "Thank you. I love you and am glad we got to share this together even with you traveling. My first time to Vegas has been worthwhile."

 Clink and smiles.

"That makes me happy to hear. I feel so bad being stuck in presentations all day while you have to find something to do. I'm ready to go home. I can't take this place anymore. The air is just...I think it's making me sick. And my boogers are starting to get hard."

"All those people packed into one area...you're bound to get sick. Just don't get me sick."

"I would never do that."

"Like you have a choice?"

"My body knows what I want it to do."

"That's enough of that."

 We break light into our room a little before midnight. I'm exhausted and fall on the bed. J-Bird grabs the lingerie she brought for the trip, and heads into the bathroom. I strip to my boxers and lay on top of the tropical flower printed bed cover. We're going to have sex. Get your shit together, Meyer. She deserves some effort.

The light from the bathroom silhouettes J-Bird against the darkness, revealing the lofted curves of her hips. She said she was going with the soft number tonight.

"Come here."

J-Bird slowly walks to the bed, I'm assuming for sexiness purposes, and gently lies on top of me. I abruptly roll over and take the top position.

"Mmm...soft and blue."

"You like it?"

"You should wear it to SIA tomorrow."

"Your accounts won't mind?"

I nibble at her neck and lift off the piece. "You, my dear, were just wearing next season's hottest piece."

"Matty, it's Jon. Give me a call back on your lunch break. I got news you'll want to hear."

I quickly put my phone back in my jeans pocket. It's raining, but not hard enough to deter me from walking the eight blocks to Tully's. I patronize Tully's for two purposes: It's not my apartment and has Wi-Fi.

"Thank you."

And the smoothies. Jesus. That's a big smoothie. Has to be eight bananas in this thing. The barista returns to the counter, and continues her conversation with the other barista about how much of dick Artie is, and that he'll probably get fired soon enough. Poor Artie's friend is playing devil's advocate, and is getting annihilated by the girls. Cut your losses, boss.

My phone's screen lights up. It's Matt. I grab it and head out into the rain to avoid any potential flack from the sisters.

"Duder."

"So what's this news? What happened?"

"A couple of things. Let's start with the shitty one first. I got fired. Helly Hansen requires my services no more."

"What?"

"Yup, my boss' territory got shrunk and I'm the recipient of the latest ax. I still get my commissions though. Actually looking at job openings now."

"That sucks, man. You liked that job, didn't you?"

"I don't know. I wasn't in love with it, and I'm going to use this as an opportunity to get into something that I really want to do."

"Photography?"

"Maybe."

"Well, you'll be fine. You're a Meyer. You're dad has grilled you enough over the years that there's no way you won't succeed."

"That's right. You don't come out of the Bill Meyer School of Business without at least a minor in resiliency."

"Well, everyone here at the bank believes in you."

"Yeah, how is the bank? Your boss still sending you gay porn?"

"Nope, he just slaps rainbow stickers on my car now."

"That's fair. So when are you leaving your posh pad in Santa Barbara for rainy Seattle?"

"I don't know, man, we'll talk about that in a second. What's you other news?"

"Oh yeah. It finally happened. Me and Angie."

"You and Angie! What?"

"Penis and vagina."

"No way!

"Yeah, man. We made out a couple of weeks ago and then last night, just kind of happened."

 Pause.

"How was it?"

"Pretty awful actually. It was not a seamless act of love. Very robotic, not much emotion on her end. I felt like I was losing my virginity all over again. I thought I knew how to please a woman."

"Angie *is* very demanding."

"But there is a positive that came out of this, or at least a positive note for Angie."

"Oh yeah, and what's that?"

"Her...you know...area. It has no smell. No smell at all. Not bad. Not good. Nothing. It's like vanilla, no wait, vanilla has taste. I don't know, think of something completely neutral and that's Angie."

"Switzerland."

"Exactly."

"Do you think Swiss chicks have smelly boxes?"

"I don't know. There is a lot of fresh air in Switzerland. If not, their tourism department is doing a great job."

Artie's buddy hurries out of the shop. No visible scratches, but definitely beaten.

"So what's your news, Matty?"

"I am officially in a relationship."

"With the chick you met up with in Vegas?"

"Yeah, Tyler. She's pretty cool, man, and a freak in bed."

"Well that's all you need. OK, give me stories."

"So she had to go to the doctor the other day, you know, her box doctor, so we couldn't have sex."

"Sure."

"So I'm lying there the other night, trying to go to sleep, and I notice she's restless and wide awake.

I inquire why, and she says she was just going to wait for me to go to sleep so she could masturbate."

Pause.

"Wow."

"I know."

"I know you know. I want to know. So you guys fucked?"

"Yeah, three times."

"I don't think that's healthy."

"Well, it happened nonetheless."

"Aside from my disappointment in respecting the doctor's wishes, congratulations on the relationship. She sounds like a cool chick."

"What's this, are you already coming back to promoting the committed world?"

"I wouldn't go that far. You know what they say though, spreading yourself around just isn't as fulfilling."

"Who says that?"

"People who fuck a lot."

"Sounds like you got some thinking to do."

"Need to find a job before I have time to think. I'm going to get back at it."

"OK, bro. Take it easy."

"Will do. I love you."

"I love you too."

I park across the street from J-Bird's in my usual spot behind the white van that is always halfway up the curb. I don't think it's moved in a year. The neighborhood trees have bloomed, offering shade to the block. Roosevelt is busy so it takes a couple of cars before I can run across to her walk. Delilah's waiting at the door, not barking. That's a good sign. She remembers me. The door is unlocked and I pet Delilah to calm her down. J-Bird turns off the TV. Leslie looks up from her Sudoku.

"Hey, girls."

"Hey, Jon. How are you?"

"All in all, not bad, Leslie. How 'bout yourself?"

"I'm OK, just getting ready for some Leslie time, you know."

"Yes, I do know. Ready to go, J-Bird?"

"Yeah."

J-Bird looks good. All it takes is a little makeup for her to be lights out. She's wearing a pair of Leslie's jeans, and a red top I've never seen.

"See ya, Les."

"Have fun, you guys."

Fun—that would be nice. I open the door and let J-Bird pass through. We take the stoop stairs together in stride, and I reflexively reach for her hand. Before my right hand makes contact, I retract it back and into my pocket. What the fuck was that? Jesus. That wouldn't have gotten things off to a good start. J-Bird guides me to some park up north I haven't been to yet. She's agreed to try hanging out.

The weather is souring as we pull into the parking lot. Puget Sound is in full view with Bainbridge Island off in the distance. The wind has picked up. People are leaving.

"You want an extra-long sleeve? I still have some samples in here."

"Sure."

I put my beanie on and get out of the Element. I pop the trunk and grab one the women's sample bag, and dig for a base layer piece. I hold it up for her viewing.

"What do you think?"

"That will work fine."

She gets out of the car and stands beside me. J-Bird quickly slides on the extra layer, and zips her fleece back up.

"To the beach?"

"Lead the way. You know where you're going."

We cross a bridge that takes us safely over some train tracks. Sand is being whisked into mini-tornados. Even though the sun is out, the wind is making the late afternoon uncomfortably cold. Our shoes sink into the moist sand. We walk the beach, fighting the wind for only fifty yards before settling down on a washed up piece of driftwood.

"So I called you because I wanted to talk to you, well...to apologize. Apologize for the way I handled things in my apartment. I should have brought my dissatisfaction, rather concern, about the relationship, to you before making such a drastic decision. I still do think that for me, I made the right choice, but I feel awful for the way I carried it out."

J-Bird continues her stare at the water. Wind whips her hair to and from her face.

J-Bird begins slowly, "It's hard for me to stay mad, Jon. After about a week, I calmed down and started rationally thinking about it. You did handle things poorly, but now I think I understand where you were coming from. I've been talking with my parents and the Meganhardts, Phil in particular, and he said that he wasn't ready for full commitment until he was thirty with Nieve."

Thank you, Phil.

"And that all the way through his twenties he doubted their relationship. Now, after being single this last month or so, I've kind of realized that I needed to be single too. With graduation and everything else going, I really need to focus on me. It was also your first time breaking up with someone that you actually had a serious relationship with. I've done it twice and have more experience. You'll do better the next time."

Thanks, I think.

"So where do we go from here? I leave it to you. Obviously, I have no right to request any kind of friendship, but I still consider you the person I've been the closest with."

"Closer than Matt?"

"Matt and I haven't had sex...yet."

"Right."

"Really though, I still care about you and value your opinion above others. You're the only one who calls me out on my shit, and I need that. Otherwise, I just get real d-bagish and that's no good for anyone. It's selfish, it's very selfish, but I still want to hang out with you. And I don't mean sex. Just in your presence. Just able to hang out like before, but without the commitment."

"You know how it is with me though, Jon. You're either in my life or out of it, and right now I can't say I want to see too much of you. If we continue to hang out and things get comfortable, we'll never be able to move on. And then what happens when one of us does meet somebody they want to pursue?"

"I hear what you're saying. It makes sense. I just know on my end I can do the friends thing. I've done it before and had it work."

J-Bird shakes her head, answering, "I don't think I can do it, Jon. It would be too hard."

"OK. It's your decision and of course I respect that."

She wraps her arms across her chest for warmth, and it's all I can do to resist rubbing her shoulders. Friends. Not lovers. Friends do rub shoulders, but not after breaking up two weeks ago.

"I'm freezing. Can we leave?"

"Yeah, yeah. Let's get out of here."

I edge alongside the curb, and put the car in park outside J-Bird's. The block is dark and quiet. J-Bird reaches for the door handle.

"So just call whenever you want to do something. I'm not going to call you, or I'm going to try to not call you. But I do want to see you, J-Bird."

"Jon...maybe. Give me some more time. I don't need this right now."

Hear that? You are being rejected.

My chest feels like it's imploding. Moisture fills my eyes. I try to put words together as tears start to drain down both cheeks. Why?

I blubber, "OK. I just don't want...to hurt you, J-Bird. Through our whole relationship...I never wanted to hurt you."

J-Bird continues to sit motionless, not sure what to do.

"I wouldn't bring things up, like Portland, because I was afraid that it would upset you, and I can't stand to see you sad."

As quick as they came, the tears dry.

"What other things did you not bring up?"

"Does it matter?"

"If you can't be honest with me now then we'll never be anything again."

Deep exhale.

I confess, "I stopped loving you before our one year. I never told you because I didn't know what to think. I still wanted to be with you, but how do you tell someone that you know loves you deeply that you don't love them anymore? At first I just thought it was us flattening out, but the doubt grew into something more."

"What's that supposed to mean?"

"What Phil was talking about. I got the twenty-four-year-old itch to be single and spread myself thin. It's different when you walk down the street and see an attractive girl. I can pass that off as fast as she walks by. But when I have to go into shops and engage with them because that's my job—realize that they have personalities, talk and laugh with them—it got to be too much."

"Too much what? Too much guilt?"

"It's because of that feeling that I had to break up with you. I couldn't take it anymore. I felt...feel...awful. To be with you but thinking about someone else. Is that fair to you?

"This is a little different 'fair' than we were talking about the other day."

"I know. I had to break up with you somehow, and I tried to go with the least painful route. I'm sorry."

"How can I ever trust anything you say from here on?"

"I don't know. I'll always put your happiness above my honesty. I can't help it. I'm a pleaser. I just can't stand to see you sad."

"Well you won't have to see me for a while. Good-bye, Jon."

Leaving me alone J-Bird snaps the door handle and jumps out of the Element.

"Whatchya' up to, Jonny boy?"

"Just hanging out. You know me. Don't do much of anything else these days."

"Want to come over tonight? Watch a movie or something?"

Think. What do you want?

"Sorry, Angie. I'm going to stay in tonight. Do a big job search push tomorrow."

"All right, well don't forget we're going out on Thursday before I leave for Peru."

"Of course. Wouldn't miss it. I'll talk to you on Thursday."

"All right, love. Sleep tight."

"You too."

JANUARY 1ˢᵀ / 2006 / SEATTLE

That was nice. Our lips separate from each other, taking in the moment. Tonight is the night. The crowded living room is cheering in the New Year. I grab my bottle of champagne, swig, and pass it to her. She does the same and passes it back.

"Happy New Year, Angie."

"Happy New Year, Jon."

Smiling, I lose focus of Angie and take in the scene. All around us, former classmates and friends are hugging and kissing in celebration. It's our first New Year away from college, and we're finding safety from the real world with one another. Someone turns the music up, blaring hip-hop throughout the house. A line of girls leaks into the living room from the hallway. One of the bathrooms must be out of toilet paper. I grab my empty red cup from the side table.

"I'm heading to the keg."

"OK."

Liv and a couple girls I don't recognize are having some deep conversation in the corner of the kitchen. I want to talk to Liv, but I don't think I could hang with them at this point. In fifteen minutes I will be officially drunk, and after this next cup of beer will be en route to bad decision making. I use my last coherent decision to avoid them, and avoid any embarrassment. It's Angie tonight. Focus on Angie.

Gee's posted up at the keg and is filling Rado's cup when I arrive. The bags of ice on top of the keg have melted, and water slowly drips off the rim to the linoleum floor. I wrap my long arms over their shoulders.

"Meyer, what up?"

"Nothing much, fellas. Everyone having a happy New Year so far?"

"You know it. Gee's about to get his groove on."

"I didn't know talking in first person was allowed after midnight."

Gee answers the question with a mini-exhibition, shuffling his feet with no discernable skill.

"Like the sweater-vest, Rado. Class."

"Thanks, Jonny. Means a lot coming from you."

"Well, you're welcome. Red really brings out the curls in your hair."

I grab the tap dangling from the keg, slant my cup, and begin filling it with whatever cheap, light beer is inside the silver shell. Gee's not getting the space he needs to dance in the living room, so he saunters back to Rado and me.

"What do you guys think of playing a little game after Meyer's filled up?"

"What came would that be, Gee?"

"The game that everybody wins!"

"That sounds like trouble."

"I agree with R.J. I think I'm already there, Geezer."

"You don't know where *there* is, Meyer. I know what you're thinking, and don't worry about it, Angie's going to be around for you at the end of the night."

"If you say so. Ready, Rado?"

"Yup."

The three of us raise our full cups of beer in a salute, and promptly begin chugging. Most nights we would be gulping as fast we could, but I get the feeling that the other guys don't want to spill. We are wearing the best stuff in our closets. Gee finishes first, followed by myself and Rado. I breathe out and wipe the excess moisture from my mouth. All three of us are staring at the ground, waiting for the inevitable belch. It comes. This draws attention from other conversations.

"I love the game that everybody wins."

"Here, here."

"OK, then. Fill it back up!"

Back in the living room, Angie and Andrea are sitting on the couch in the corner. A guy from Gonzaga, I remember his face but can't place a name, is next to them with some Everclear. I exchange quick pleasantries while sliding through the crowd. Lots of people I haven't seen since graduation. I plop between Angie and Andrea. Familiar face takes me in, not looking too flustered by my presence. He means no harm.

"Hey, man, you want some Everclear? Brought it in from Canada."

"No thanks, this is the last beer for me tonight."

"Angie? Andrea?"

Angie reaches for the bottle, "Sure," and takes a pull. I can smell the alcohol emitting from the mouth of the bottle. My stomach turns. Angie hands the bottle to Andrea and settles back into the couch, obviously waiting for the immediate effect. Her thin frame goes limp.

I ask if she's all right, and after a moment she perks back up.

"Yeah, good."

"Good."

Jack's standing by the door holding two cigarettes, motioning to me.

"I'll be back. Going to have a smoke with Jacky."

"You don't smoke."

"I know."

It's cool outside, the lights of east Queen Anne sparkling across Lake Union. Jacky lights his cigarette, then hands me his lighter. With scary fluidity, I light mine and take a long drag. The smoke expands in my head, making me a bit dizzy. We kill half our cigs before Jack inquires about Angie.

"I think tonight's the night, man. Been some time coming, but I think she's finally over Adam, and I've got nothing going on, except for a friend of a friend at Helly, so why not?"

"Sounds like a plan, Stan."

"Barring any accidents, I don't see why it won't happen."

"You ready for it? This has been a long time coming. Sure you don't want to call Matt?"

"When it actually happens...that's when I call Matt. No sooner, no later." I take another drag and point my finger at the ground. "Like right when I come, that's when I call Matt."

Jack's chilled breath mixes with our cigarettes' hazy smoke. "Sounds like you have it figured out."

"Like I said, it's been a long time coming."

We flip our roached heaters off the deck, and before I look back to the house I hear Andrea yelling my name. Jack and I look at each other, shrug, and return inside. We find Andrea in the hallway.

"What's going on?"

"Angie's puking out front. Are you ready to go?"

Not tonight.

"Shit, yeah...that's fine. Out front? Is she still there?"

"Yeah, we're all there. All the girls."

"All right. See ya, Jacky."

"Good luck," Jack says with a smirk, disappearing back into the living room and the noise while I follow Andrea out of the house. Huddling around a puking Angie are Ashley and Liz, rubbing her back. The front of house light illuminates the yard, creating shadows from the bent over girls. Tupac's lyrics rain over the neighborhood. Must be the alcohol. This is a sad situation.

"Girls, ready to go?"

Ashley interlocks arms with Angie.

"Are you OK to move?"

Angie nods. Ashley and Liz insist on carrying her when I could easily sling her over my shoulder. They're the roommates. They can have the responsibility. We hurriedly walk the two blocks to the Escort, and place Angie shotgun. I roll her window down for the drive home in case she's not completely empty. The rest of us are going to have to deal with the chill.

Back in Wallingford, I piggyback Angie into the house, and onto her bed. The girls congregate to the booth in the kitchen to rehash the night. In her bedroom, Angie mumbles something about me staying over. I nod, roll her on her side, and settle onto the familiar couch in the living room.

The waiter leaves our two Guinnesses on the table, and resumes watching the door in case anyone else should happen to come in. Empty booths line the window. Refreshing.

"Thanks again for meeting me, Lyndz. I just have a ton of shit in my head that I need to run by you. You're always objective and even though I know you really like J-Bird, you'll be honest with me."

"Well, you have to be honest with me first."

"I know. I know."

"So what's up? Obviously something is weighing you down if you're calling me in. What'd she do?"

"It's not her. She's done nothing wrong. She's been great...actually. It's all me and my fucking head. I can't stop thinking about being single again...the temptation."

"What brought this on?"

"All the time in the car with nothing else to think about. Having to stop into shop after shop with cool, hot chicks interested in what I do. It's different when you have to talk to them. Girls on the street keep walking on by. Out of sight, out of mind. But these girls are always there, every month, every trip, still there."

"So you're thinking about other women—that's no big deal. Your relationship is strong enough to pass that off."

"I don't know, Lyndz. I'm sure by now you've heard that I'm thinking about moving to Portland."

"Yeah, to make the driving easier."

"Right, well what the move was also going to serve as a little break from J-Bird. A gap. Some time to really figure out where we're going while still together. The problem is from the beginning, I've always thought about her staying up here, never moving down. Worse, I wouldn't want her to come down."

Lyndsay postures back, cupping both hands around her beer.

"Oh."

"I know. So let's say I move to Portland but am still dating J-Bird...would it be wrong to ask a girl on a date in Portland?"

"Yes."

"Really?"

"Yes, Jon. Are you crazy? If that's the way you feel, you need to break up with J-Bird. Have you talked to J-Bird about the move?"

I look away in preparation for the next admittance. The head on my Guinness has fizzled a bit. I take a sip and set the pint back down.

"We kind of had it out today."

"What happened?"

"We were just running errands around Ballard. Stopped into Fred Meyer for some lunch and she asks me if I've ever thought about moving. I wonder how she could be reading my mind because all I can think about is this move and whether it's going to happen or not. That and how I'm going to bring it up. Why would I want to tell her I'm thinking about moving when nothing is for sure yet?"

"Jon, have I taught you nothing? Girls always want to know what's happening even if it's just going to the store."

"Maybe I should have had you tell her. So we got into a big argument in the Fred Meyer deli about how she's part of this relationship too, and how could I not consider her feelings? That's all I'm considering. I guess just in the wrong way. What happens if I tell her I'm moving, and then don't go? Then she thinks I'm trying to get away from her, and it *just didn't work out this time*."

"Aren't you?"

No.

"I think what I'm looking for is an easy way out of the relationship."

I lay my hands open on the table, framing my beer.

"This is what I have on my plate: Someone that I care deeply about, love as a friend, and somehow I have to tell her that I don't want to be in a committed relationship anymore, but would still love to see her on a regular basis because I still want her in my life. Every word of that is honest. I just have this deep inner yearning to be single again. It gets worse by the day."

"Jon...you have to cut her loose. What you're doing is not fair to her. If you're thinking about seriously dating other girls, like hooking up with them, you shouldn't be in a relationship with J-Bird."

That makes sense. Lyndz is right.

"OK. That's what I needed to hear. I needed someone else to say it."

"Glad I could help, but I like you two together. She's good for you."

"Not making it any easier, Lyndz."

"What are friends for?"

"Telling friends that they need to break up with their girlfriend."

"That's a little dark."

"Hasn't been a great week."

MAY 29TH / 2007 / SEATTLE

Rain bounces off the blacktop of the Queen Anne Elementary basketball courts, giving the smooth surface a dark shine. Some of the guys are already shooting, making the most of it. T-shirts are starting to soak through. Water splatters after every dribble of the ball. I park the Element and hop out into the late May drizzle.

"Gentlemen."

"Good to see the rain didn't scare you off, Meyer."

"Come on, Gee, you know I'm good to show."

"Where's Hern?"

"Not sure. Probably on his way. Rado?"

"Same."

"Hope we get fours."

"Yeah."

Gee tosses me the ball and I chuck a jumper that catches the front of the double rimmed hoop. The ball splatters on the ground and goes dead like it just lost all of its air.

"Looks like we're going to have to dribble extra hard today."

"Yup."

"So you guys going to Angie's thing on Thursday?"

"Don't see why not. Not like my life has anything better going."

"That's positive, Jacky. How about you, Scotty?"

"Where's it at?"

"Ozzie's, I think."

"Yeah, I'll go then."

"Good, she'll appreciate it."

"You know what else Thursday is, Meyer? May 31. The final night."

"Oh, I know, Gee. This shit is coming off first thing Friday morning. No more dodging cops for me."

Gee and I dance with each other in the contemporary style of a hybrid robot, looking at the ground with arms extended. The rain will not deter us. Scott and Jack start shooting again, doing their best to ignore us.

"Twos until the others get here?"

"Sure."

"Sounds good."

"Let's shoot it up, then."

Gee and I break our trance, wander to the top of the three-point arc, and form a broken line. Rain comes down harder. Puddles are now forming on the court. Jack lofts a shot that hits the back of the rim before going in. I step to the line and take a dribble.

"So what's going on with that SPU chick, Meyer?"

"Yeah...that."

My chest is hurting again. I shove the letter away so my tears don't drip onto the pages. I've already rewritten it three times. I don't want to have to rewrite it again after finally getting down what I think she needs to hear. Get your shit together. Make the call.

"Hey."

"Hey."

"So can I come up to your place?"

"Why would you do that? The Element's still in the shop, right?"

"Want to meet halfway, then?"

"Why don't I just come to your place?"

Because it's shitty to have you come over here for me to break up with you, and then have you drive home. I think it's rude.

"Um...OK. That's fine."

"See you in a few."

"OK."

Fuck.

I'm leaning against my bedroom door frame when J-Bird enters. I'm waiting for her the same I way I would when she'd come over after her shifts at the hospital. The letter is in my hand.

"It's easier for me to write, but you know that. I'll answer any question you want."

J-Bird takes the three pages out of my hand without taking her eyes off mine, and sits down at the computer desk. I move to the kitchen and lean on the counter, and wait for the inevitable eruption. Her eyes dart across the pages, but reveal nothing from within. Once finished, she throws the pages on the desk.

"You really want to break up? You have to be fucking kidding me! That's pretty rash, Jon."

Calm. Act calm. You've thought this out.

"I've been thinking about it for a while. It's not like this is a spur-of-the-moment type of thing."

"And once again you don't feel the need to tell me that, what, let's see here, you don't love me anymore? Never felt like something you might want to bring up?"

"It's the first time I've gone through anything like this, and I wanted to make sure I knew what I was feeling and that I made the right decision. That took time to figure out."

"So you were just waiting for it?"

"It's not like that. To me, we've hit a plateau the last four months. I can't help but think of you more like a friend at this point."

That sounds stupid.

"Well that's what good relationships are...friends who happen to be a little more."

"So friends with bennies?"

"Don't be stupid. Do you still love me?"

I cross my arms, preparing for the blow.

"Not anymore."

"Is this because I brought up Portland yesterday?"

"No...kind of...it made me think about things a little more seriously. I don't know if I'm moving to Portland yet, but I think it's a problem that not only did I not want to bring it up with you, I don't want you to come with me. Don't you think that's a problem?"

"I think you put too much weight in the effect your decisions have on me."

"Maybe I do, but nonetheless...what happens if I go to Portland and you come, and then we break up? I'm going to feel guilty as hell because I brought you down there, and then we're both stuck."

"I have a choice too, Jon. If I went it's because I wanted to go. Not just because you're down there. Who says I'd go to Portland anyways? I have things I want to do here."

"Personally, I'm not ready to be responsible for someone else's major life decisions. Maybe I overvalued your commitment?"

"Enough with the financial language!"

"I can't fucking help it, J-Bird. This is how my dad..."

"I know, I know. Your dad never had emotional conversations with you, and now you have a hard time with these things. I know, Jon."

"I'm sorry, but I saw serious flaws with the fact that I didn't want you in Portland if I was in Portland."

And the fact I want to go on a date with a certain girl in Portland.

"You want some water?"

"No."

"You want to sit on the bed? It's more comfortable."

"No, Jon. I don't want to sit on your fucking bed. I want a straight answer."

J-Bird stands from the chair, snatches the letter, and heads for the exit. We meet at the door.

"Do you want to be single? Do you want out of this relationship?"

"If you read the letter..."

"Do you want to be single?"

Yes. I'm sorry. Be honest. For the first time be honest. You can't protect her. You can't lie to her. You have to be honest.

"Yes."

J-Bird opens and shuts the door, taking the stairs quickly. I open the slammed door and yell down the stairwell, "Please read the rest of it!"

"What's the fucking point? Leslie will be over in fifteen minutes with your shit!"

Ozzie's is slammed for a Thursday. The karaoke downstairs is in full force already and it's only ten. People fill the bar from front to back, occupying every bar stool and pool table. Jeff and Swan are at the top of the stairs waiting for the bartender. Other random Gonzaga heads bob up and down over the crest of the second-floor wall. Quite a good showing. Nobody I know is downstairs, so I ascend to the second level. A pre-bar forty would've gone a long way tonight.

It seems Angie's going away party has turned into the once-a-year gathering of GU alum that decide to all go out together, and pretend we're all still incredibly great friends. The horseshoe of red booths bustles with postgrad conversations about employment, housing, and school loans. There's Moopy, flirting with every girl hoping that one will find him amusing and then eventually parlay it into a blowy. Gee is in the corner with Laura and Jack. Theanne is looking as good as ever. Liv is even making an appearance. I sneak up on the boys.

"What are we drinking, fellas?"

"Mr. Meyer. Good to see ya."

"And you two too...yeah, that makes sense. What a crowd tonight, huh? I feel like we're back in the Logan neighborhood and I should be starting to formulate odds on who I have the best chance of going home with."

"Some things never change."

"Contrary to your comment, Jefferson, I don't plan on going home with anyone tonight."

"But what about the single life? What about being young and having as much sex as possible?"

Jeff drops his hand on my shoulder, wedging his fingers around my collarbone.

"A life I know little about."

"So humble."

"More like realistic. Have you guys ever taken a girl, a stranger, home from the bar in Seattle? Let me answer for you—no. No one has. It's impossible. I have a better shot at discovering a newfound math formula than hooking up with a girl from a bar."

"One can always hope."

I obtain eye contact with the bartender.

"And one can also drink. Mac and Jack's, please."

"So what happened, then? No more Angie? J-Bird? That girl that nobody knows? That other girl that nobody knows?"

The bartender hands me my beer and asks, "Open or closed?"

"Open, please."

I take a sip, letting the cloudy ale expand in my mouth. My body relaxes.

"Nope. None of them."

"I don't understand."

"I don't either. Still trying to process what's happening. Not normal. I've got to get back to Ellensburg for a couple of days to work it out, I think."

"Why Ellensburg?"

"I've found I think a lot more clearly there. Not so many distractions. Just the valley, the mountains. Home."

"You're bringing me down, Meyer. I'll catch ya later."

Swan raises his beer to head height while using his free arm for balance while shuffling away through the crowd.

"Yeah, sorry, Jeff. I don't mean to...I don't want to talk about this shit anymore. It is depressing. What do I have to complain about?"

Lack of job. Lack of direction. Lack of...

"That's it, man. Jeff, listen. I think guys our age, we're not necessarily looking for a serious girlfriend, I think we're looking for more of a...a...companion. Some chick we can hang out with, hook up with, and...I don't know what the fuck I'm saying. Never mind."

Jeff's hand moves from my collarbone to my shoulder, and he pulls me into a half hug. The movement shakes some beer loose that finds its way to my shirt.

"I'm sorry, man, but you gotta take it easy."

"No big deal. I have a million shirts with a million pockets."

"Oh, what? I was talking about the girl stuff. How 'bout you come with Uncle Jeff and we'll go talk to some cuties. Remember all those times we've said how we're going to hit the town and meet some new people—girls? Tonight's that night."

"I don't know, Jefferson, I think I'm just going to take it easy on this one. My head needs to get straight before I engage with another female. Seriously, don't let me hook up with any chick. Seriously. Tonight, it's the path of least resistance."

Eleven o'clock. Gee has already done his *Return of the Mac* karaoke performance, which, of course, brought the house down, and I've all but avoided conversations regarding my lack of employment. Dim lighting keeps the atmosphere chill. Angie's thin frame slides through the crowd and sits down in the booth I'm now sharing with Jack and Jeff. She's wearing a nice little black top that I'm sure she bought with Lyndsay on one of their excursions. When she wants to look good, she looks real good. Angie's cocktail finds the table after a couple of tries, and comes to rest next to my two empty pint glasses. She's drunk. I'm on my way.

"Hey, fellas."

"What up, Angie? Going with the 'hung-over flight is the best flight' theory?"

"Is there any other?"

"I actually prefer the 'stay up all night and sleep on the plane' theory. You know the alcohol smell emitting from your body is what makes people's faces scrunch when you sit down next to them, not your outfit comprised of sweaty articles of clothing."

"People love my travel outfits, Jonathan."

The table snickers. Jeff changes the subject.

"You going to be wearing that outfit down south? I hear Peruvians love cotton."

"Should I feel like I need the attention."

Angie's chin quickly drops.

"Yes...but I don't think that will be a problem. My hombres know I'm coming and will have their catcalls ready."

"Does it ever get lonely up here in the States not having someone whistling at you while walking down the street?"

"Only when I think I look really hot, Mr. Jack. You American boys usually express your delight with free drinks. Am I right?"

We take in the invitation, but no one accepts.

"Unfortunately, I believe so. Chicks suck."

Jack's cheeks are getting rosier—a rant is coming on.

"You girls come out to the bar, sometimes without wallets, or purses, whatever the fuck you girls carry, expecting to get bought drinks with no intention of going home with a guy. It's not even playing the game, it's...it's...disgraceful. God, is that the only word I can come up with?"

"And that's why I never buy girls drinks."

"No, Meyer, you don't buy girls drinks because you're cheap."

"This is true."

"You've bought me a drink before."

I raise my eyes from the half drunk beer in my right hand.

"Let me rephrase. I don't buy a girl a drink that I don't know."

From my end of the booth I can see the top of the stairs and the numbers lingering around the bar. With the low light, things are turning a little hazy. Leslie and Lyndsay emerge from the bar with what must be vodka-crans. I slide out of the booth and stumble my first couple of steps, adjusting to my newfound state of drunkenness.

"Excuse me. I'm going to talk to Lyndz and Leslie for a minute."

Nods from the booth. Most everyone's attention is on Ashley who's making out with some guy from GU that I don't recognize in the back booth. Wow...they're really going at it. I turn back to Lyndsay and Leslie who are leaning against the booth closest to the bar, and J-Bird slides out from the lingering mob to Leslie's side.

That's interesting. Looks like she just got off a shift. Her hair is still wet and she's not wearing any makeup, but still looks great in jeans and a gray tank that wraps around her hips perfectly. I saunter across the room to the girls, and they must be picking up on my intoxication because I'm getting some raised eyebrows. I hear Lyndsay mention Ashley, leading me to believe that they weren't talking about my staggering steps. That's nice.

"Ladies, how are we?"

"Doing good, Jon, how are you?"

"I'm great. J-Bird, a pleasure. You just get off?"

Don't be a fucking dick.

"Yup. Snuck out a little early."

"Save any lives tonight?"

"Nope, just held a lot of babies."

I lean in, lowering my head, I offer one of our inside jokes, "The baby whisperer."

"Yes, I am the baby whisperer."

That gets a smile. There it is. Make her laugh.

"Do you guys want to take over Ashley's booth?"

"Sure."

The four of us sneak up on the event taking place in Ozzie's most coveted corner booth, and Lyndsay taps on Ashley's leg that is poking into the common area. Ashley's head swivels away from the mystery man.

"I'll trade you cab fare money for your booth."

Ashley rattles her head and seems to come to a realization—maybe one that says she shouldn't be making out with this guy in the corner booth at Ozzie's.

"That won't be necessary, Lyndsay."

She faces back to her accomplice.

"I'm done for the evening, James. Until next time."

Ashley rises and checks herself out. Asking for respect back, she straightens her top, and briskly walks off, leaving poor James still lying in the booth on his back. I reach a hand out, which he takes, and help him up.

"Sorry, buddy."

"Where'd she go?"

"Around the corner."

"Fuck it."

We watch James walk straight to the bar and start talking to another girl. Now boothed, J-Bird and I catch up while Lyndsay and Leslie gossip about the store. My intoxication has leveled off into a steady buzz. My focus is holding. I inquire about J-Bird's sister's love life.

"So Kidda and Jake still together?"

"Yup, doing well. Now he's going to SPU. We'll see how it goes."

"SPU? What happened to U Dub?"

"I think he wanted something more religious. I don't think they'll last the summer."

"Right."

"Your parents?"

"Fine. Getting along. Not that they ever haven't. Bill's working on the office merger and Rosemary is worrying about her boys. Nothing that new."

"She sent me an e-mail."

"Who?"

"Your mom."

Okay.

"Why?"

"Congratulating me on graduation. It was very nice."

That woman. Why am I surprised?

"Is this how we're going to be from here on out? General questions? Catch-up talk? Nothing deep ever again?"

"I think so, Jon. Yes."

"Huh. Yup. Probably a good idea."

My cell phone says it's 12:30. I bid adieu and bounce my way out to the downstairs bathroom, dodging pool cues and flailing arms. Jeff's beer stain on my shirt still hasn't dried up. I push through the crowd. Someone starts in on *Sweet Caroline*, but is really murdering it. That's too bad. The front door opens, letting in a handful of people. Some dudes, some girls. I see some points coming my way followed by index fingers forming mock mustaches. What do they know of commitment?

My attention is averted from their snickers when A-bomb slinks out of the crowd. I don't understand. She never comes to Queen Anne. What is she doing here? Can I magically levitate back to the second floor, and the safe bubble of my fellow alumni? Can I teleport? How have they not come up with this technology yet?

A-bomb recognizes me, and smiles. She motions to her friends to stop making fun of my mustache. Friends that I've only heard about and never met. I don't want that to change. I make a move for the stairs and inevitable interaction.

You're a bit drunk.

You can do this.

My right hand goes for the railing while my left is grabbed by A-bomb.

"Hey."

"Hey. Um, what are you doing on Queen Anne?"

"I'm here with my friends for someone's birthday. One of those things. How about you?"

"Going away party. Lots of GU kids. Upstairs."

"Cool cool. Well what are you doing afterward?"

No sex. No.

"I can't."

A-bomb's eyebrows synch together and I think she mutters a, "Huh?"

I blabber, "I can't hook up with you anymore."

My left hand drops free.

"Um, what's going on, Jon?"

"I can't do it. It's fucking with my head too much. I'm sorry, A-bomb. It wasn't a good idea to begin with and it's my fault for initiating. I'm sorry."

Sweet Caroline finishes, making way for *On Bended Knee*. I love this song.

A-Bomb's eyes fall to the ground and her head slowly motions back and forth. "It's not like I want to date you or anything...I don't know what I want. I don't understand."

"I'm sorry. I'm just trying to find...something. Something else. I'm sorry."

I take the stairs, leaving A-bomb openmouthed and motionless. At the top, Jeff is waiting and embraces me.

"Who was that?" He says while looking over my shoulder.

"That? That was mystery girl number one."

"She looks pissed."

"She has a right to be. I told her I don't want to see her anymore."

Jeff's definitely drunk. All smiles.

"No shit! You're a mercenary, Meyer. Fuck me."

"There will be no fucking tonight, Jefferson."

"Ain't that the truth. You know what you need?"

Absolutely not, I have no idea what I need. Someone that could tell me exactly what I need, right now, would be heaven sent. I would follow them anywhere.

"No."

"A beer."

"How bout two?"

One o'clock. People, lights, thoughts are all blurring together. I'm hanging onto Jeff. He's spilled on my shirt again, this time on my left shoulder, but instead of awkward looks I'm now getting humored sympathy. Gee's leading the room in a sing-along of *Bohemian Rhapsody*. Angie's dancing wildly in the middle of a crowd, surrounded by rando guys looking to poach territory. I'm not the man to stop them tonight. J-Bird is nowhere to be seen, keeping any underlying temptation absent as well. No chance to say something incredibly idiotic. Time to go home.

"I'm out."

"Huh?"

"I'm leaving. Thanks for the company, Jeffery, but it is time for me to retire."

Oversize arms pull me in for one final hug.

"I'll see ya later, Jonny."

"Yes, you will."

i break into Angie's dancing circle to say goodbye. Her dirty blonde hair stops bouncing when she feels my hand above her hip.

"I'm outta here. Be safe and come home...eventually."

For the second time in as many minutes, I'm grasped into an embrace. Just under Freddy Mercury's voice I hear Angie say, "I'm going to miss you so much," and I pull away.

"Right. OK. See you when you get back."

The blonde hair begins bobbing again.

I close out and leave through the back.

JUNE 1ST / 2007 / SEATTLE

My throat. My head. Yikes. I look to the side of my bed, and, just as I had hoped, rests a pint of water. I push up on my right arm, and with my left grab the glass. I chug it, in one gulp, and instantly feel better. Shower.

Cleansed, I wipe the fog from the mirror. I can hear Moopy's snoring over his TV. It's time. I pull on each side of my cheeks, preparing for the not-so-comfortable shave about to happen. My mustache has filled in nicely, but it's time to go. Application of the shaving foam is key. I usually like to highlight my chin and neck slots, as those are most likely to receive a cut, but today the upper lip gets all the attention. Look at it. Closely. Little porcupine spikes jutting out from a snowfield. Brown wheat grass rising from Cool Whip. A month's worth of attention-grabbing, socially questionable, facial hair.

Gone.

The distance between my upper lip and nose has increased it seems. That's odd. Stroking my chin, I look in the mirror at a person unfamiliar to me.

10682121R0

Made in the USA
Lexington, KY
12 August 2011